A Family Departed

A Jason Thompson Medium Mystery

Wayne M. Utter

D1523169

For Terri, Who Has Always Believed In Me.

Contents

Chapter 1

"They're not your family!...they're all dead!" Lisa Bowen had reached her limit.

"Lisa, wait! Please don't leave. You don't understand." I tried to make my fiancé see my point of view, but she wasn't buying it.

"I understand that our relationship is going nowhere!" she shouted. "Jason, I love you, but we've been engaged for 3 years, and you refuse to set a wedding date. You know, if we got married, we could start our own family. A real family, not a bunch of dead people!"

Lisa and I have been together for 5 years, including the 2 years that we dated before getting engaged. 5 years is a long time. I don't want to throw away 5 years of our lives. Lisa is the love of my life. At least, I think she is. Who knows? I'm not sure what love is. She has always been there for me. Lately, though, things have been different. I don't know how to describe it...just *different*. Lisa wants to get married and have kids. I keep stalling, and it pisses her off. I love her, but I can't picture her as the 'motherly' type. At least not to my kids. She is more of a career type of woman who wouldn't have time for kids. As Village Clerk of Ventura, Illinois, she puts in a lot of hours. Her father, James, is mayor, and has been for the past twenty years. Lisa plans on running for that position when her father retires next spring.

As for me, I'm far from perfect. I suffer from acute anxiety, relying on medication to get me through some rough days. The only music I'll listen to is country. Not the crap they play on the radio today, but real, traditional Country Music. And I'm obsessed with genealogy. It's my hobby, and all I have left of my family. The Thompson family tree ends with me, unless I have children. The only Thompson left in the phone book is me, and the only 'family' I have is six feet under the Ventura Cemetery. They're all I have, but Lisa doesn't understand that. She has a big family with lots of living relatives. Brothers, sisters, parents, grandparents, aunts, uncles, cousins. Every year, the Bowen family reunion gets bigger and bigger, and every year Lisa becomes furious with me because I bring my laptop and log on to Ancestry.com. *My* family reunions stopped when I was a kid.

So this was another typical Thursday evening at my apartment. Lisa comes over every Thursday and we order takeout. Most weeks it's either pizza or Chinese, a bottle of wine, some country music playing softly in the background, and some pleasant conversation. After dinner, we would either have great sex or we would get into a terrible argument. This week was General Tso's Chicken and no sex. She wasn't even going to spend the night. I can remember when we first started dating. We were like rabbits, unable to keep our hands off each other. We had sex nearly every night of the week. I always use protection, though. Lisa insists she is on the pill and I don't need to worry, but I just don't trust her memory. Kids are great and I look forward to becoming a dad, but only when the time is right. Until then, I'll be cautious.

"Jason, please think about what I've said. If you can't let go of the past, there can be no future for us."

We had been through all of this before, but she had never been this upset. Letting go of the past is difficult for me. So many of my family members had passed away under questionable circumstances. Accidents, fires, heart attacks in very healthy people. The deaths in my family just made no sense. One by one, family members died unexpected deaths. None of my family members died of old age. They never got to that point. But if I attempt to talk with Lisa about it, she calls me a paranoid conspiracy theorist. *Whatever*. I don't have it in me to argue anymore.

"I'll call you later, ok?"

Lisa looked at me with tears forming in her eyes. "Okay," she whispered. Being overdramatic, she lowered her head, turned and strolled toward the door. I think she was expecting me to get on my knees and beg her to stay. Tomorrow is another day, though. Lisa will never apologize, but she'll be fine tomorrow. Argument?...what argument? As Lisa left, I tried to figure out why someone with her looks and brain would want to be with me. Lisa could pass as a model. She's 28, blond hair, blue eyes, a killer body, and a smile that could melt a snowman's heart. I was no slouch, though. At 6'2", 200 lbs, short brown hair, and mostly clean-shaven (I keep a very thin mustache), I definitely look younger than my age of 32.

After Lisa had left, I fired up my laptop and logged on to Ancestry.com. Lately, it seemed like I had more questions than answers regarding my family tree. Genealogy research usually opens more doors than it closes, and that's what keeps it interesting. If you run into a dead end on one branch, move on to the next. Answers don't always come easy.... Sometimes they never come at all. Again, that's what keeps it interesting. Their names on my laptop screen made me feel closer to my ancestors, although I never actually met any of them. They had all passed away before I was born.

Around 11:00, I called Lisa to make sure she made it home safely.

"What are you doing?" she asked.

"Nothing."

"You're working on your family tree again, aren't you?"

I paused before answering. "Maybe."

"Jason, let it go. Your family is gone, and you can't bring them back. Concentrate on the present and the future. Let's start a family of our own."

"You're probably right, babe." I always called her 'babe' when I was tired of arguing and wanted it to stop. Sometimes it worked. "We can talk about it more this weekend, ok?"

"Okay Jay. Now turn off your computer and get some sleep.

You have to go to work in the morning!" Lisa sounded like the mother I wished I still had.

Chapter 2

The next morning, I was awake early. It had been another restless night, with odd dreams and very little sleep. Seeing people I've never met, and listening to them speak of unknown places night after night, makes it very difficult to get a restful night's sleep. But there was no time to dwell on it. There was work to be done and money to be made.

My daily commute to work comprises a 5 mile drive from my hometown of Ventura to Menderville, Illinois. The mileage on my 2005 PT Cruiser is less than 100,000 miles, and a tank of gas lasts me two weeks. My job is awesome. I work for my best friend, Kyle Butler, as a dispatcher for one of the largest trucking companies in the Midwest. Kyle is every single girl's heartthrob. At 6'4", 230 lbs of pure muscle, dark complexion, and long wavy hair, he could have any girl he wanted in Crandall County, and he's had quite a few of them. Butler Transportation has offices and depots in 5 states, and we have well over 50 tractors and 100 trailers. We deliver everything from donuts to scooters to furniture, and everything in between. I make decent money, never break a sweat on the job, and Kyle puts no pressure on me. If I screw up scheduling a delivery, he always covers my ass and tells me not to worry about it. Who could ask for anything more?

"So, how was the sex last night?" Kyle asked me the same question every Friday morning. Maybe I share too much with Kyle, but I need someone to talk to, and Kyle always listens attentively, especially when I tell bedroom stories.

"No sex. It wasn't a good night."

"That sucks. Is she still on your case about setting a wedding date?"

"Yep. That and some other things." I didn't want to get into it any deeper with Kyle, because I've never discussed my love of genealogy with him. I'm not ashamed of it, I just don't care to share all of my family history. It's very personal and should be kept private.

"Well, you know I'm here for you."

"I know, and it is very much appreciated." Kyle has *always* been here for me.

As I got back to scheduling deliveries for Monday, Kyle's cell phone rang.

The look on his face told me it wasn't good news. "Did you make your delivery yet?" asked Kyle. Whenever Kyle asked that question, it meant there was a problem with a truck or a driver. Or sometimes both.

"Ok, leave your GPS on, so I can find you. Yep, I'll drive a tractor to you and we can make the delivery. I'll call a tow truck when I get there, to have your tractor towed to a repair shop. See you in a few hours." Kyle hung up and put his cell phone in his shirt pocket. "Damn it! I wanted to get out of here early today." Kyle was angry, but this is why his trucking company was so successful. He always put the customer first.

"That sucks, man! Anything I can do for you while you're gone?" I knew what his answer would be, but I had to let him know I had his back.

"No, just hold down the fort. I should be back by 5:00."

"Don't worry, everything is cool here. Drive safe, ok?"

"Always do," said Kyle as he ran out the door.

The rest of the morning was very busy. Phone calls and on-line orders for full trailer and LTL deliveries took up most of my time. With Kyle out of the office and most of our drivers on the road, I could listen to my favorite music. George Jones and Merle Haggard sounded great on the stereo that Kyle had bought for the office. At 11:45, I called Tony's Pizza to order a Chicken Parm Hero for lunch. Tony has the best Italian food in town, and the fastest deliveries. I was already looking forward to a nice, peaceful lunch, as our answering service would take the phone calls from 12:30 to 1:00.

At 12:15, I was completing some Bill of Ladings, and someone appeared in the corner of my eye. "Wow, that was fast. I didn't even hear you come in. Set it down anywhere. How much do I owe you?" There was no answer. As I turned to get a better look at whom I thought was the delivery person, the room went dark and the stereo was silenced. It was the strangest thing I ever saw. I have 2 windows in my office, and the blinds were opened on both of them. Yet the room was pitch black, not a bit of light anywhere in the room.

"What the hell happened!?" I yelled out. There was no answer.

As I fumbled through my desk drawer for a flashlight, a voice became noticeable. It began very distant and breathy....almost like a whisper, but slightly louder. I couldn't make out who was speaking or what they were saying. Could it be Tony's delivery person? "Who's there?" I asked repeatedly. The same eerie voice continued. Suddenly, the voice became louder and more intelligible.

"Jason."

"Yeah, who's there?"

"Jason."

"Yes, that's me. Who's there?"

"Listen to me. Find a way to listen to me."

"Okay, I'm listening. What do you want??"

All at once, the lights and the sound system came on again. Standing before me was an old man. He had gray hair, a long beard, and was wearing clothing circa 1950s. He scared the hell out of me, and my first instinct was to back away from him. When I did, my desk chair caused me to lose my balance, and I fell to the floor. There is no carpeting in my office, and landing on a hard tile floor hurts like hell. While sitting on the floor, a voice came from the other side of my desk.

"Dude, are you ok?"

Slowly getting back to my feet, I replied, "Who are you?" The old man was gone, and now a teenage boy stood in front of me.

This young man was very blurry, though. The fall must have messed up my vision.

"I'm Vince, Tony's my dad. I'm just delivering your lunch."

"Oh, Ok.Where did the old man go?"

"What old man?" Vince looked at me curiously.

"The old man that was just standing here. He was there when the electricity came back on."

"The electricity?? Wait, what are you talking about? I've been standing here for 5 minutes, trying to get your attention, but you've been staring out into space. There's been no old man, and the electricity has been on the whole time. Are you sure you're ok?"

"Physically, I'm fine....but there's some weird shit happening here today." I had two 20 dollar bills in my wallet, so I gave one to Vince and told him to keep the change. The quicker he was gone, the better. I needed some time to collect my thoughts. I was sure there had been an old man standing in my office. Pretty sure anyway. His face looked so familiar. Had I met him somewhere before? Maybe he was one of our drivers? No, I definitely would have remembered seeing him around the depot.

I kept myself busy the rest of the afternoon. Anything to keep my mind occupied. I even cleaned the bathroom.

True to his word, Kyle walked through the office door at 4:55pm. "Not bad, huh? I made damn good time!"

"Not bad at all. Kyle, have you hired any new drivers recently?"

"Yeah, I hired a kid to be our new yard jockey. He just got his license and doesn't have any experience. He's going to start work on Monday."

"No old men?"

"Nope. What's wrong with you? You look like you've seen a ghost!"

Maybe I had.

Chapter 3

"Jason, did you see me? Did you see me in your office?"

"Who are you?" I asked.

"You know who I am."

"No...no I don't. Tell me who you are!"

"Find the truth, Jason, before it's too late...."

I woke myself up, yelling and kicking, the sweat pouring off my forehead.

"Jay, wake up! You're dreaming again....wake up!" Lisa said as she held me tight.

"Ok, I'm awake. I think I'm awake. Am I awake, Babe? I can't tell."

"You're awake Jay, but you scare the hell out of me every time you dream."

"I'm so sorry Lisa. Are you ok?"

"I'm fine, but maybe you should see a therapist. These dreams aren't normal."

"I already see a therapist. I don't think there is such a thing as a *dream therapist*."

"Sure there is...they're called 'psychoanalysts'. And who is Caleb?"

"Caleb? I don't know. Why do you ask?"

"You were calling out his name in your sleep."

Lisa fell back asleep, but I was no longer tired. I got out of bed, put my robe on, and went to the kitchen for a snack. It was only 3:00am, but I knew I'd be up for the duration. Might as well have a sandwich to keep my mind occupied. Ham, Swiss, liverwurst, onions, and mustard on rye bread should do the trick. And a big glass of milk.

Suddenly, it hit me! Caleb....Caleb....Caleb Thompson! My great-grandfather's name was Caleb Thompson. Born 1895 — Died 1953 - Buried in the Ventura Cemetery. The brakes on his pickup truck had failed, and he wound up drowning in Lake Menderville. Don't ask me how I remember stuff like this. I guess it's so many hours of research, and so many miles of walking through area cemeteries. I was told by my father that Caleb had purchased a brand-new Ford F-100 two weeks before the accident. Brakes failing in a new vehicle doesn't make sense, but anything is possible. I guess.

Caleb's wife (my great-grandmother) Flora, also had a suspicious death. She was 55 when she passed. 2 to 3 mile hikes were normal for her. Yet, she tripped on a rake in her garden and hit her head on a rock when she fell to the ground, killing her instantly. But if I mention any of this to Lisa, she tells me I'm a paranoid schizophrenic. Some things are better left unsaid.

*   *   *

"What *are* you doing?" Lisa asked skeptically. She was getting dressed and preparing for a day of shopping in Peoria with her mother and sister.

"I'm looking for an old photo album that my dad gave me," as I dug through some old cardboard boxes buried deep in the hall closet.

"Oh, sounds fun," she said sarcastically. "You didn't get much sleep last night."

"No, I'll probably take a nap later."

"Ok, well enjoy! We'll be gone most of the day, so I'll call you tomorrow, ok?"

"Ok Babe.....have fun! Love you!"

Lisa didn't reply as she hurried out the door.

Chapter 4

My apartment is not very big. It consists of a bedroom, living room, bathroom, eat-in kitchen, a very narrow hallway, and two tiny closets. It's small but affordable, and it's easy to keep clean. Just not much storage space.

After Lisa left, I pulled all the boxes out of the hall closet and lined them up on the living room sofa. After opening and examining the contents of each box, I returned them to the closet.

Finally, as I searched the contents of the sixth and final box, I found the photo album. It was old and worn out, had a brown leather cover, and the pages were plain black paper. You had to use the glue on photo corners to attach pictures to the pages. As I flipped through the pages, I found photos of my grandparents, aunts, uncles, and even a shot of my dad when he was a young boy. A tear ran down my cheek as I looked through the history of a family departed, that was no more. Each page made me long for a family that I didn't know very well. Most, I only knew by their tombstone. The last page of the album contained the photo I was searching for.....the only known picture of my great-grandfather, Caleb Thompson. As I moved into the light to get a better view, I froze in disbelief. Holy shit....HOLY SHIT!! The man in the photo was the same man that was standing in my office yesterday! And the same man who was in my dream last night. How was this possible?? How was any of this possible? Had I seen this photo before? I must have if I knew where to look for it. But I don't remember ever seeing a photo of Caleb. If it wasn't for a tiny piece of masking tape with the inscription "Caleb T." written on it, I wouldn't have known who it was.

So, as badly as I have always wanted to know my family members, now I'm not sure if it's the right thing to do. I'm scared, he's scared. What are we so afraid of? He spoke to me, and I listened....so why did he tell me to find a *way* to listen to him? And why do I have to find the truth before it's too late? Too late for what? Oh boy, what a time to run out of my anxiety meds. Maybe I should call Lisa. No, she would just shake her head in disbelief and tell me I'm imagining things again. Too much to think about for one morning. I needed sleep. Lots of sleep.

I tossed and turned on the couch for over an hour, but couldn't sleep. My mind was racing, my heart was racing, and all I could see when I closed my eyes was Caleb Thompson standing in my office. He only appeared briefly, but I'm positive it was Caleb. Now, what do I do? What does he want? Who can I speak to about him? Maybe I can just call him and he'll appear out of nowhere?

"Caleb!......Caleb!....Are you here? Can you speak with me? Can you tell me what you want?" Boy, do I feel like a jerk. Calling a ghost and expecting him to just show up. I think I *might* be losing it.

I took 2 melatonin capsules and went back to bed. Trying to function on just a few hours of sleep, with my brain working overtime, wasn't going to happen.

*   *   *

The satin sheets of the Peoria Grande Hotel's bed felt so good on Lisa's naked body. And the weight of a muscular man on top of her felt even better. She didn't enjoy telling lies, especially to her fiancé, but sometimes she had to. There was a lot at stake.

"Don't forget to use protection, baby! I have to bear Jason's children. It's very important!"

"Don't worry, I will," said Kyle Butler as he paused to put on a condom. "It's important to many people." Kyle didn't like sharing Lisa, but hoped he wouldn't have to do it for much longer.

Chapter 5

Caleb Thompson loved being a farmer. He enjoyed the feel of freshly tilled soil in his hands. He loved the way it smelled. And he loved feeling the warm summer sun on his face and arms as he worked the fields. God had been very good to Caleb. After working tirelessly for other people, for many years, Caleb had saved enough to purchase his own land. So, in the winter of 1939, he bought 90 acres of fertile land bordering Roberts Creek. It was only 90 acres, but it was enough to give him a good start on his lifelong dream. He began his endeavor with some very basic equipment. An Oliver Cletrac and a Ford 8N were the first tractors he purchased. Onions, corn, lettuce, pumpkins, and hay were the crops he raised. He did most of the work himself. Flora would help when she could. She was a schoolteacher and a darn good one. Small in stature, but huge in heart, she took immense pride in what she and Caleb were accomplishing with their lives. Her days consisted of teaching, grading homework and test scores, staying after school to give extra help to kids that needed it, and spending time with Will. Will was Caleb and Flora's only child. They loved him dearly and were extremely proud of him. During the school year, Will was a straight-A student and a star athlete. But during the summers, he worked his butt off on the farm, spending 12 hours a day in the fields. The Thompsons were not wealthy, by any means, but they enjoyed a glorious life and were thankful for everything they had.

In the spring of 1944, Will graduated from Ventura High School with honors. He was offered a full scholarship to play baseball for The Fighting Illini at the University of Illinois. Caleb and Flora wanted him to accept the scholarship, but knew he wouldn't. One week after graduation, he was on a train headed to Fort Sheridan for boot camp. His first responsibility was to his country. Will had enlisted in the US Army, and would spend the next 14 months hunting Nazis in France and Germany. He fought bravely and won many commendation medals. After the war, he stayed in Berlin for a year to assist in the rebuilding process.

Will came back to the farm in the summer of 1946, finding a tranquil life waiting for him. Several nagging combat injuries prevented him from continuing his baseball career. But that was ok with Will. He was just happy to be home. Caleb and Flora were ecstatic that he came home to Ventura. It meant the world to them. It meant that they were back together as a family.

The next three years, the Thompson Family Farm flourished. Caleb and Will handled the backbreaking work, and Flora took care of the business side of the farm. Profits doubled and then tripled, and by the planting season of 1950, they were able to purchase an additional 30 acres adjacent to their current property. This acreage was in back of their existing land, and was separated by a dense grove of trees. This meant they would have to hire extra help and purchase some new equipment, but the economy was good and they could afford it. After this, things really took off. Will married his long-time girlfriend, Mary Kallas, and together they bought their first house, with dreams of starting their own family. If they only could have seen what was about to happen.

Chapter 6

I finally woke up a little after 6:00pm, and surprisingly, I felt much better. I still didn't understand exactly what was happening in my life, but if it meant a chance of getting to know my ancestors, then it can't be all bad, right? The first thing I needed was a shower, and then some food in my stomach. I had eaten nothing since the night before, and I was starving. After shaving and showering, I decided to drive to Menderville and eat dinner at Tony's. I could really go for a big plate of Tony's baked ziti. Tony made his sauce from scratch, used homemade pasta, and added mozzarella, ricotta, and cottage cheese to his pasta dishes. The taste was out of this world!

Upon arriving, Tony's parking lot was surprisingly empty. Then I realized it was almost 8:30pm. Apparently, the dinner rush was over, and things had settled down.

"Jason! Welcome! Come in and sit wherever you want," Tony yelled excitedly when I walked in.

"Thank you, Tony. It's nice to see you again!"

"You as well, my friend. Tell me, where is your lovely fiancé this evening?"

"She's doing what she does best. Spending money!"

Tony laughed and patted me on the back. "What are you drinking this evening?"

"I'll have a bottle of Michelob, please."

"You got it, Jason. Have a seat, and I'll be right back with your drink!"

I sat down at a small table next to the front window. Tony

had a way of making everyone feel at home. His restaurant was nothing fancy. The red and white plaid tablecloths, soft lighting, and Frank Sinatra music playing on the stereo, was enough to bring in a decent size crowd almost every evening.

Tony returned a moment later with my beer. He twisted the cap off and poured it into a tall, frosted glass.

"Thanks Tony!"

"You're very welcome, sir. Do you know what you want to eat this evening?"

"Yep....no need for a menu. I'll have the baked ziti, please."

"Ahhh...excellent choice, my friend! I'll have it ready for you in a few minutes. Oh, by the way, what happened to you yesterday?"

Not knowing exactly what Tony was referring to, I asked what he was talking about.

"Well, you called and ordered a sandwich, but my delivery girl went home sick. I had no one else here to deliver it. I tried calling you, but there was no answer."

"Oh, no problem, Tony. Your son brought it to me."

"My son?"

"Yep. Vince is a very polite young man."

Tony looked at me with a cold, hateful stare. "Is that supposed to be some kind of joke?"

"Is *what* supposed to be a joke? What are you talking about?"

"I think you'd better take your beer and get out!"

"Tony, what did I say?? Please don't be angry...Tell me what I did wrong!"

Wiping a tear from his cheek, Tony said softly, "You don't know? You really don't know?"

"I swear Tony! I don't know what you're talking about."

"Jason, my son Vince, died in a car accident almost 3 years ago. A drunk driver killed him while delivering pizzas. I don't know who was there yesterday, but it couldn't have been my son."

"Oh my God, Tony! I am so sorry. I remember hearing about a young man getting killed in an accident, but I had no idea it was your son. The past 2 days have been very strange. Shit has been happening that I can not explain."

"It's ok Jason. Forgive me for getting upset with you. Sit here and drink your beer. I'll have your dinner ready in a few minutes, ok?"

"Thanks Tony."

As Tony headed to the kitchen, I tried to replay the events from the previous day in my mind. I remembered seeing Caleb, and falling on my ass, and when I got up Caleb was gone. In his place was Vince, or someone claiming to be Vince. I pulled out my wallet and gave him $20.

So, I pulled my wallet out of my pants pocket and unfolded it. Inside were two $20 dollar bills. The same number that were there yesterday, before I paid Vince. So, I guess I didn't pay him. But now that I think about it, I can't remember eating lunch yesterday. Maybe I imagined the whole thing? Maybe I hit my head when I fell and knocked myself out? I don't know... I'm not sure. I'm not sure about anything.

When Tony returned with my dinner, I ate half, and asked for a box to take the leftovers home. It had been a long day, and I just wanted to go home. Before leaving, I shook Tony's hand and apologized again for bringing up unpleasant memories. He assured me that everything was fine between us, and said goodnight.

*   *   *

Tony got on the phone as soon as the taillights were gone.

"Hey, it's me. I don't like the way he's acting. Yeah, he thinks Vincent was in his office yesterday. I think we should do something before he gets suspicious. I know we have to handle this one differently than the others. Shouldn't be a problem, though. Ok, talk with you soon."

Chapter 7

1950 and 1951 were good years for the Thompsons. They were blessed with pleasant weather, great crops, and many wonderful family times. Will and the hired men handled the manual labor, so Caleb could take on the role of farm manager. Mary assisted Flora with the paperwork and billing, which gave Flora the opportunity to devote more time to teaching. Things couldn't be better.

In the spring of 1952, Caleb's neighbor, Thomas Bowen, paid a visit to the Thompson Farm. Caleb found it odd, because he and Thomas had never been more than casual acquaintances. Nevertheless, Caleb offered a friendly handshake and welcomed Thomas.

"Good morning Thomas. Beautiful day, isn't it?"

"That it is, Caleb. That it is."

Thomas Bowen had a reputation as being the meanest, greediest, nastiest man in Crandall County. Money was all that mattered to him. He knew how to make it, and how to spend it. And he was never satisfied with what he had. There were some who said he would do *anything* to increase his fortune. Thomas had inherited 100 acres, a house, a barn, and a few old tractors from his father. Little by little, he built his farm empire. Through buyouts, takeovers, and shrewd business deals, he became the wealthiest and most powerful farmer in Illinois.

Still curious about the purpose of Thomas's visit, Caleb smiled and asked, "To what do I owe the pleasure of this visit?"

With a disdainful look in his eyes, Thomas pointed to the line of trees at the back of Caleb's original acreage and said, "I want to buy your fields on the other side of those trees."

Caleb looked astonished and replied, "Now why would you want to buy those fields? You already own over 500 acres."

"I need to grow more corn. I just signed a contract with a local distributor."

Caleb became more curious. "What distributor would that be?"

"Umm.... I don't think you would know them. They're from Des Moines."

"But I thought you said they were local?"

"Well, they have a local office. I think it's over in Aaron."

Caleb calmly and confidently looked Thomas in the eyes and pronounced, "Thomas, my land is not for sale. Besides, you have more than enough acreage to handle any fictitious contract with a distributor that doesn't exist."

"Are you calling me a liar, Caleb?"

"What I'm saying is, I know every buyer and distributor of produce in Illinois and Iowa. There are no distributors in Des Moines, with offices in Aaron."

"I'm willing to pay you top dollar for that land!"

"Sorry, it's not for sale."

"Ok, but if you change your mind...."

"I won't." Caleb cut him off before he could say another word.

Thomas got into his truck and left in a hurry.

Caleb was completely stumped as he watched him drive away. It made no sense. Thomas wanted that land, but wouldn't say why. Maybe Thomas was being semi-honest, and he really did need more land? It wasn't likely, though. The Bowen family was wealthy and powerful, and they were used to getting their own way. There had to be a good reason Thomas wanted this land so badly. So Caleb hopped on his tractor and drove down to the back fields to take a look around.

Chapter 8

Sunday came and went with no phone call from Lisa. It didn't bother me, though. Sometimes I preferred time away from her. Maybe, if she could accept me for who I am, things would be different. Maybe I'd be better off without her. Or maybe I should just take my anxiety meds and quit overthinking things.

After another night with little sleep, I knew I had to do something. An early Monday morning call to Kyle was a surprise to him, and to me. In the 7 years I've been working for Butler Transportation, I can count the number of times I've called out sick on one hand. But this call was different. I wasn't just calling out sick; I was asking for some time off. When Kyle asked how much time I would need, I didn't know what to tell him. A week? 2 weeks? A month? Who knows? Kyle was supportive, as he always was, and told me to take as much time as I required. He didn't know why I was asking for time off, but he respected my privacy, and didn't require me to explain.

At 10:00am, I called my therapist, Dr. Ken Phillips, and asked if he had time to see me ASAP. 1:30pm was the best he could do. Actually, it was faster than I expected, so I was happy with that. It gave me some time to lie on the couch and take a little nap. I have the world's most comfortable couch. I love taking naps on it. Sometimes I'll fall asleep and spend the entire night on my couch. It's also pretty good for having sex on, but that's a story for another time. Today, I was tired and comfortable, and I drifted off to sleep quickly. Just as I was about to start snoring, my phone rang. Damn it....it never fails. I sat up and looked at my phone. It was Lisa.

"Hello?" I said coldly. I wanted to let her know she woke me up, and I wasn't happy about it.

"Hey Jay, is everything ok?"

"Yeah, why wouldn't it be?"

"Well, your car was parked in the driveway this morning. I just wanted to check on you to see if you're feeling ok." That was a lie. Lisa never goes past my apartment on her way to work. She must have been speaking to one of her nosy family members.

"Yep, I'm feeling great! Just needed a day to myself." If she can lie, then so can I.

"Ok, okay. Well, if you need anything, just call me, ok?"

"Sure thing, Babe. I'll talk to you later."

I ended the call quickly because, honestly, I just didn't want to speak with her. It's so strange to be in love with someone, but not being able to, and not wanting to, communicate with that person.

I stretched out on my couch again, determined not to be disturbed a second time. A rerun of Judge Judy was on the TV, but I only heard it briefly as I drifted off to sleep.

Suddenly, I found myself walking up a long dirt driveway with a row of trees on each side. Pine, I think. Maybe spruce. I can't tell the difference. Seems the faster I walked, the longer the driveway became. I walked what felt like a mile, and finally, in the distance, two stone pillars appeared, one on each side of the driveway. As I reached the pillars, ahead there were tombstones. That's when I realized where I was…. The Ventura Cemetery. I had been here many times, doing research on my family tree. The weather was cold, damp, and windy. Leaves were blowing around the tombstones, but the only trees in the area were evergreens. Ahead of me was a woman dressed in black, clutching a handkerchief. She was crying…. The kind of cry so heartbreaking, it made me want to cry too. I approached her and asked what was wrong. The sobbing didn't stop, and soon she was joined by a second woman, also crying. A third and fourth also joined them, all wearing black dresses, stockings, hats, and veils. They all held hands and formed a circle around me. I stood in the center of this circle, but was not afraid. Actually, I felt protected. It was obvious, at this point, that we were all there for a funeral.

"Ladies, please forgive me for having to ask, but can you tell me who has passed on?"

They all spoke together in unison....almost in perfect 4-part harmony, "You should know, Jason. We've been trying to warn you. Find someone to help you before it's too late."

I awoke with a start, and this time found myself not sweating, but crying. The throw pillow on my couch was soaked with tears. I had been crying like the four women I had just seen in the cemetery. Why??? Why would I be crying? Was it my funeral? Who were these women? At least one of them looked very familiar, but I just couldn't place where I'd seen her before. Maybe in an old picture? I should pull out my photo album once more. Maybe I'll get lucky again and find an image of her. But, it will have to wait till later. It was already 12:30pm and Dr. Phillip's office was in Milan, a good 30-minute drive from Ventura.

A quick shower, and I was out the door at 1:00pm, just in time for Lisa to pull into the parking lot and park her car next to mine. Lisa jumped out of her car and came at me like an NFL linebacker. She grabbed me by the back of my head and pulled my face to hers.

"Oh Jay, I've missed you so much. We haven't done it in over a week," she said, before she thrust her tongue in my mouth. "I have a few minutes before I have to get back to work. We could have a quickie!" she suggested, with a devilish grin on her face.

"I'll have to take a rain check, sweetie. I'm late for an appointment."

"Oh, come on...don't you have a few minutes for me?"

"Sorry Lisa, I can't. I have to go."

"But where are you going?"

Maybe I'm crazy, but it almost seemed like she was more nosy and less compassionate with that last statement. "I have an appointment with Dr. Phillips."

"Why? I thought you were doing ok with the medication he prescribed?"

" I thought so too, but it doesn't seem to be working as well as it did. Maybe he needs to adjust the dosage."

"Just don't let him over-medicate you. I don't want to be engaged to a zombie," Lisa grinned.

"So, I'll see you later?" I asked.

"You can count on it, baby. Tonight, you're all mine," Lisa purred in a very seductive tone of voice.

Chapter 9

James Bowen ruled Ventura with an iron fist. The grandson of Thomas Bowen, he had been the mayor for nearly twenty years, and treated the village like his own personal property. Before being elected mayor, he was chief of police for fifteen years. James felt it was his civic duty to run an authoritative village government, and to constantly remind the citizens of Ventura that he was in charge. He got away with it because almost half of its residents were related to him. The Bowen family was enormous, and getting bigger all the time.

Ventura Village Hall was actually an old Victorian home, passed down by a deceased member of the Bowen family. No expense was spared in the restoration of this building. The exterior was decorated in a handsome gray and white color scheme, with a dark charcoal colored roof and wraparound porch. The interior featured hardwood floors, and a unique color combination for each room. Central air, Wi-Fi, and a stereo sound system were some of the modern comforts that had been added in recent years. Lisa and her father shared a large office on the first floor, just across the hall from the front door.

"You're late Lisa. It's 1:05!"

"Sorry daddy, I won't let it happen again. I wanted to check on Jason."

"That's not an excuse. In fact, there is no excuse for tardiness." James expected nothing less than perfection from his daughter. If he was going to hand over the reins to her, she would have to prove she was worthy to be mayor. "So tell me, how are things between you and him?"

"They're great! Couldn't be better! I really believe we'll be setting a wedding date soon. Everything seems to be falling into place!" Nothing could be further from the truth, but it was easier to lie than to listen to another scolding from her father.

"Good. Just don't disappoint me, Lisa. You know I hate being disappointed."

"I know, daddy. Don't worry....just leave it to me, ok?" Lisa craved love and respect from her father, but seldom received any. Instead, she lived in fear of his temper, and his desire to control her life.

Lisa's mother had died when she was a young girl, so her father was the only parent she had ever known. It wasn't easy, always trying to live up to his lofty expectations, but Lisa did what she was told. She knew that someday she would be in control of Ventura, and a few other things that would make her one of the wealthiest women in Illinois. Until then, she lived a pretty good life. She made decent money, had good benefits, and still lived at home with her dad, living rent-free. Her job also offered her many opportunities to meet rich, handsome men from around the area. To Lisa, it was just innocent flirting, however the flirting sometimes went a bit too far. As long as Jason didn't find out, though, things were good.

*   *   *

"So, what can I do for you today, Jason?" asked Dr. Phillips.

"You can tell me I'm not going crazy, Doc."

Doctor Phillips chuckled, "That bad, eh?"

"I think I need some stronger medication."

"Well, suppose you tell me what's going on, and then we'll decide if you need stronger meds, ok?"

Doc Phillips had a nice, cozy office with overstuffed furniture, a fireplace, and a variety of houseplants. If he had a big screen TV installed, it would be the perfect place to watch a Cubs game on WGN. Oh well, you can't have everything. The recliner looked like the best place for me. Lying on the couch always made me feel like a basket case.

I told Dr. Phillips about my visits from Caleb and Vince. I also told him about all of my dreams, including the most recent one involving the crying women.

"So, what do you think? Is this anxiety, or am I just going crazy?"

Dr. Phillips had been busily taking notes while I was speaking. Or was he just engaged in a good game of Sudoku, hidden in his notebook? "Jason, what do *you* think it is?"

I paused and thought for a moment before I answered. "I know it sounds crazy, but this is real! I *know* my great-grandfather was in my office. And my dreams have never been so vivid."

Dr. Phillips paused for a moment while he finished taking some notes. Finally, he said, "These are not symptoms of anxiety. And even if they were, you take 20 mg of Celexa daily, which should be enough to take care of your anxiety. No, there's something else going on here."

"Oh boy, I was afraid you were going to say that. Level with me, Doc...what's wrong with me?"

Dr. Phillips reached for his cell phone. After scrolling through his contacts, he looked me in the eye and said, "I'm sending you contact info for a friend of mine. Her name is Tina White. I want you to call her."

"What is her specialty?"

"Oh, she's not a specialist." Dr. Phillips finished sending the contact and gave me a reassuring smile. "She's a medium."

"A medium?" I replied.

"Yeah.... you know, she talks with spirits. Communicates with the dead...stuff like that."

At first, I felt offended. "Is this supposed to be some kind of joke?"

"Joke? No, I wouldn't joke about something like this."

Now, I was really confused. "I didn't think people like you believed in the spirit world."

"People like me?" the doctor chuckled. "What do you mean by

that?"

"No offense, Doc, but you're a doctor....a man of science. Don't your ideals contradict what spiritualists believe?"

"Jason, the human spirit is an incredibly powerful entity. Our bodies are frail. They don't live for very long. 70, 80, maybe 90 years if you're lucky, and that's it. Bury them or burn them after that. But, our spirits live on....forever."

I was seeing a side of Dr. Phillips that I didn't know existed. "You amaze me, Doc. I never would have guessed you held these beliefs!"

"Jason, my mother passed away a few years back. We were very close, and it hurt like hell to lose her."

He paused for a moment, as tears began forming in his eyes. I felt such empathy for this man. I wanted him to continue with his story. This really hit home with me.

Dr. Phillips continued, "Mom wasn't a churchgoing woman, but she was good...very good! It's unbelievable how many people she helped in her lifetime. After she passed, I had a lot of sleepless nights, thinking how unfair life is. I mean, here's a woman who spent her entire life helping her friends and family. So she passes away, and that's it?? I kept rehashing it over and over. There had to be more."

"So you went looking for a medium?"

"Hell no! I thought mediums were full of shit. That is until I met Tina. She was one of my patients."

"Weren't you afraid she was a whacko?"

"You're one of my patients....are you a whacko?"

"Point taken, Doc."

Dr. Phillips continued, "Tina and I became friends. She's a kind lady who has a personality much like my mother's. After opening up to her about my grief, Tina told me she is a medium, and would like to help me connect with mom."

"I assume she made that connection?"

"I'm not going to say anymore, Jason. Don't let my experience influence your outcome. Call her. Maybe she can help you. In the meantime, keep taking your medication, and try to get some sleep."

"I'll do that. Thanks for your help, Doc."

Chapter 10

After leaving Dr. Phillips' office, I decided to stop at the Ventura Cemetery. It was a warm, sunny day, and I needed to check on my parents' graves, because it had been a while since I had been there. I parked my car at the base of the hill preceding the tree-lined driveway and walked the rest of the way. Upon entering the graveyard, the name "Thompson" could clearly be seen on many tombstones. As I walked to the end of the first row of graves, I came upon the stones of mom and dad. Next to them was my brother, Charlie. They had been gone nearly four years, all victims of a house fire. It was bad enough losing mom and dad, but Charlie had just graduated from Notre Dame, and had come home for a brief visit before moving to Los Angeles to take a job as an accountant. He had his whole life ahead of him. Damn fire inspector couldn't even come up with a cause of the fire. As I knelt beside the markers, I said a prayer, pulled some weeds, and had a quiet little conversation with all three of them. I missed them all so much, it hurt.

My next stop was Caleb and Flora's graves. They were in the third row, about halfway down. Because they both passed away long ago, I knew little about either of them. Dad had told me that Caleb was a farmer, but he had passed even before dad was born. The location of his farm remains a mystery, but it's really not that important. Apparently, the land was sold to pay back taxes, or so I've been told. What really matters is that Caleb wants to communicate with me, but neither of us knows how to have a conversation across the spirit realm. Maybe I *should* contact Tina

White?

After standing and stretching, I realized the weather had turned cool and cloudy, with a strong northerly wind whipping up. It was surprising because the weather forecast was for warm, sunny weather all day. As I turned to walk toward my car, the foggy outline of a person appeared several feet ahead of me. I couldn't tell if it was male or female, but I assumed it was a spirit. Dressed in black with a hood pulled over its head, it didn't speak to me, but somehow I sensed what it wanted from me. As it got closer, the spirit held out its hand to touch mine. Holy shit, I had never touched a spirit. Can you even physically feel the touch of a spirit? I reached out to take its hand in mine. The moment our hands touched, everything went dark. Just like it did in my office last week, the world became black. I pulled my hand away, but the darkness remained. This is unreal....how does it happen? It's like going into a black hole without a speck of light. Suddenly, a figure appeared in front of me....an illuminated figure on a black background. Things came more into focus. It was Caleb, but now he was joined by a second person. It was a man, much younger than Caleb. The two men were standing in a field about twenty feet away from a grove of trees. No voices were audible, but the two men were clearly arguing over something. It appeared that Caleb had just said his final words on the subject, and was ready to leave, when the other man grabbed a shovel, swung it, and hit Caleb squarely in the face with it. Caleb's blood splattered all over me, along with a few teeth. Oh, my God!!....did I just witness a murder that occurred 70 years ago??

My next vision was this mysterious murderer loading Caleb's lifeless body into the bed of his pickup truck. Fast-forward about thirty minutes, and now they are on a knoll, looking over a lake. Everything is happening so quickly! Where are the police when you need them? The lake looks strangely familiar. It's a small lake with lots of lily pads along the shore. After the murderer placed Caleb's body behind the steering wheel, he released the brake and pushed the truck just enough to get it rolling down the hill. It met the lake with an enormous splash and quickly sank to the bottom. Now I knew where we were... Lake Menderville. It looks a lot different now. I was powerless to do anything. Aside from being covered in blood, I couldn't interact with anything that was going on. It was like being in a movie theater, watching the feature presentation.

Is this how my great-grandfather really died? Maybe he didn't drown after all. Maybe it was murder. But, damn it, I couldn't get a good look at the face of the murderer. Even if I could, this was seventy years ago. Anyone who committed a murder that long ago is probably dead by now, right?

Suddenly, the light returned, and I found myself standing with my hand still extended to touch spirit's. The sun and warm temperatures had returned, and the wind had diminished. The blood was gone, and there was no sign of a shovel, a pickup truck, or Lake Menderville. And the spirit had gone too. So, did I just imagine all of this? Or does it have a way of letting me see the past? Holy shit, so many questions and very few answers. I need to call Tina White. From what Dr. Phillips said, she was my best bet for finding answers.

I looked at my watch. It was almost 5:30. Damn it! Lisa is coming over. If I don't get home, she'll worry about me. The call to Tina will have to wait until tomorrow.

Chapter 11

When I arrived at my driveway, I found Lisa's BMW parked there. I knew already that this would not go well. Upon opening the front door to my apartment, I found Lisa lying on the couch, wearing a black lace bra and panties. She was gorgeous and very sexy, but I had other things on my mind.

"It's about time. I was beginning to think you didn't want me anymore," Lisa said seductively.

"No, that's not it at all," I tried to reassure her.

"Then show me you want me, Jay."

I walked to the couch and sat down next to where she was lying. As I leaned over to kiss her, she grabbed my shoulders and pulled me on top of her.

"Wait Lisa, I need to talk to you."

"We can talk later, baby." Lisa pulled me tighter and wouldn't let go.

"Lisa, I can't right now! So many things have been happening, and I really need to talk with you."

"Are you serious, Jay? I'm offering you my body, but you would rather talk? Most guys don't....I mean, *wouldn't* turn me down!"

I paused for a minute when I realized what she just said. "And how many guys have you offered your body to?" I asked angrily.

"None! I made a mistake, Jay....I meant to say *wouldn't*! I'm sorry!"

"Whatever, Lisa. I'm really not in the mood for this. Maybe you should go home, and we can talk some other time."

Lisa looked at me with a shocked expression on her face. "You really want me to go?"

"Yeah, I think it would be best." I never refused sex before, but I had so many things on my mind, and couldn't concentrate on anything.

Without saying a word, Lisa got up from the couch and went into the bathroom, where she quickly dressed. Before leaving, she wiped a tear from her eye and said, "Call me when you feel like talking."

Lisa walked to her car and drove away. My relationship was going down the toilet, but surprisingly, it didn't bother me. I think Lisa was shocked that I stood up to her and didn't give in to her wants and needs.

After she left, it was like a weight was lifted off my shoulders. Lisa can be very intimidating at times because she is spoiled. Letting her have her own way definitely doesn't help matters. Maybe I should have stood up to her a long time ago. But enough about her. A sandwich and a Pepsi are my gourmet dinner. I need to place a phone call.

Dr. Phillips said that Tina reminds him of his mom, so I'm assuming she is an older lady. Actually, I hope she *is* older. That would mean she has more experience as a medium. More experience = better results....right? I got out my cell phone and scrolled through my contacts until Tina White's name popped up. I was nervous as hell, but this was something that needed to be done. I pressed 'Call' and crossed my fingers.

The phone only rang once when a woman with a very soft, gentle voice answered.

"Hello?"

"Hello, is this Tina?"

"Hello Jason, I've been expecting your call."

"You have?!" Holy shit, this woman really is psychic.

Tina giggled, "Yes, but only because Ken told me you'd be calling, and your name came up on caller ID."

"Oh, okay!" I laughed and explained what I was thinking about her psychic abilities.

"So, Ken said that you may be in need of a reading?"

"I think I need more than that. Can you do a reading with more than one spirit?" I asked.

"Possibly. How many spirits do you want to connect with?"

I wasn't sure of how many, so I gave a generalized answer. "My entire family."

"Oh my! Well, it's usually a one-on-one conversation, but we'll see what we can do. Why don't you come to my office tomorrow morning....say around 10 o'clock?"

"That sounds great, Tina. But first, I have to ask, how much is this going to cost?"

"Don't worry about that right now. We'll figure that out later. Google my name to get directions to my office. I'll make some coffee, and we can talk. Sound good?"

"Yep, sounds great! I'll see you then."

*   *   *

After leaving Jason's apartment, Lisa drove directly to Kyle's house, where she parked her car and knocked on Kyle's front door. Kyle was surprised to see her standing there.

"Lisa, what are you doing here? You shouldn't have come here....people will see you!"

"I don't care. I think I'm losing him."

"Come on....you're not losing him. The way you spin your web, you can catch any guy. Including Jason. Maybe he just needs a little space?"

"Maybe....but I don't want to take a chance on losing him. There's too much at stake. We need to find a faster way to end this, once and for all!"

Chapter 12

Will Thompson held his mother's hand as they walked out of the Ventura Presbyterian Church. Flora's face was pale and wet from tears flowing down her cheeks. It was just two weeks ago that Caleb had driven away from Galesburg Ford in his brand new F-100 pickup truck. He was so proud of that truck. Years of backbreaking work had finally paid off. No more secondhand junk. Caleb had finally hit the big time. But yet today was his funeral.

So what the hell had happened? Flora had been trying to get a grasp on this for the past week. Brakes don't fail on brand-new vehicles. It just doesn't happen. And why was he in Menderville? He said he was going to Aaron to buy fertilizer. He never purchased it from Menderville Feed and Grain....said they were too expensive. Even if he changed his mind and went there, it was nowhere near the lake. It just made little sense.

*　　*　　*

It wasn't easy, but the Thompson family bravely struggled on without Caleb. Will took over as manager of the farm. He was a born leader, and under his direction, Thompson Family Farm became the best run farm in Crandall County. Mary took over the business end of the farm and did an outstanding job. Neither Will nor Mary slowed down one bit. And they finally received some much-needed good news when they found out Mary was going to have a baby.

Flora went back to teaching full time. It was the only thing in her life that she loved enough to keep her mind off Caleb, even if it was only for a few hours a day. She also started hiking. Walking to and from work every day, and taking long nature hikes on weekends, kept her in shape and helped ease some of the stress she felt. Gardening was another one of Flora's hobbies. She could spend hours upon hours in her garden. Tilling the soil, fertilizing, weeding....these things brought her so much joy. Sure, she was still the owner of the farm, but it had become too large for her to perform too much manual work. Flora's garden was her private little paradise, where she could go to be alone. None of these things, though, could replace the love that she and Caleb shared for so many years.

On a beautiful afternoon in the autumn of 1953, Flora was walking home from school along Route 17. A big white Cadillac pulled alongside, and then in front of her, parking on the shoulder of the road. Thomas Bowen got out and forced a fake smile at her.

"Afternoon, Flora," said Thomas.

Flora detested Thomas and the whole Bowen family. Their love of money and material objects went against all the values that Caleb and Flora had cherished and shared with Will.

"Thomas," Flora replied coldly.

"I'd like to speak with you."

"About?"

"I want to buy some of your land."

"*Really*?"

"Yes ma'am. 30 acres on the back side of your property," Thomas smiled at Flora. "I spoke with Caleb about it, just before he passed away. He agreed to sell, but we weren't able to complete the sale."

"Funny, he never mentioned it to me."

"It must have slipped his mind. I can have my lawyer draw up the papers, and we can close on it pretty quickly."

"No, thank you," replied Flora with a smile as fake as Thomas's. Then her smile disappeared, and she scowled at him with hatred in her eyes. She continued, "Not only are you an egotistical, pompous asshole, but you're also a liar. Caleb told me about your proposition, and we both agreed that we would never, ever sell you any of our land. So get in your car, drive away, and never bother me or my family again."

Thomas got back in his car, and as he gunned the throttle, he yelled out, "You'll regret this, Flora!"

Chapter 13

T he month of May was always a busy time for Flora. Her school year was ending, her garden was blooming, and she loved to go for long walks and hikes. One overcast day toward the end of May 1954, Flora felt exhausted. After a long day at school and a brisk walk home, she just wanted to have a quiet dinner and go to bed early. A fresh garden salad had Flora's mouth watering. She already had most of the ingredients in her refrigerator, so she just needed to make a quick stop in her garden to grab a tomato and a cucumber. A 'quick stop' was just a pipe dream when it came to her garden. She could spend hours gardening and reminiscing about bygone days.

Opening the gate of her garden fence, Flora quickly spotted a beautiful, dark red Roma tomato. She knelt down to get a better look at this particular plant. It was at the end of the row, next to a rather large rock she had moved last year. There were several ripe tomatoes on this plant, so she picked all of them. While kneeling in the soil, she paused for a few moments. She could smell the vegetables in her garden. Closing her eyes, she could pick out the scents of each plant. Tomatoes, cucumbers, green peppers, string beans, radishes. The aromas were fabulous.

This is what made Caleb pursue a career in farming. He had such a great love of the land and what it could produce with a little nurturing. And this is also one thing that made Flora fall in love with Caleb.

As she sat on the ground in her garden, Flora closed her eyes and recalled their first date, their first kiss, Caleb's marriage proposal, and many other joyous occasions. What she wouldn't give, to feel Caleb's warm embrace and soft, gentle kiss just one last time. She could almost feel his hand gently stroking her soft hair. It felt so real. She refused to open her eyes, in fear of it coming to an abrupt end. Suddenly, the stroking stopped, and the hand rested on the back of her head. She opened her eyes to see if someone was actually there.

Lifting her eyelids, she slowly turned her head to the left. A figure was crouched next to her. Flora asked, "What are you...." The hand that had been stroking her hair so gently, grabbed a handful of that hair and squeezed it until Flora cried out in pain. Then, in one swift motion, thrust her head down violently on the rock next to her. A loud 'crack', reminiscent of an egg being broken against the edge of a frying pan, silenced that cry. Blood quickly drenched the rock, and tiny skull fragments were also visible.

The individual that caused this bloodbath grabbed a rake from an adjacent shed and threw it on the ground next to Flora's breathless body. This indeed made it appear to be an accident. Feeling satisfied with a job well done, the cold-blooded killer leapt over the garden fence and sprinted away without being seen by anyone.

Chapter 14

I was awake early the next morning. Nervous as hell, it felt like a first date. What should I say to Tina? How should I act? Acting naturally would probably be a good idea. But she might think I'm a freak! Oh boy....why do I do this to myself? She wants to help, so I'll tell her my story and see how things go. Checking the time on my cell phone, it was only 8:00am, so I had plenty of time to kill. Tina's office is in Aaron, which is only a fifteen minute drive from my apartment.

After pouring my first cup of coffee, I went to the hall closet, and pulled out box #6. The infamous box that holds Dad's photo album. I brought it to the kitchen table, opened the box, and found the book I was searching for. The last time I opened these pages, I knew who I was searching for. This time, I was looking for photos of women. Any women. I only got a good look at one of the ladies in my dream. The other three women kept their faces hidden. So, I needed to find any and all pictures of women in the photo album.

Slowly examining every inch of every picture in the photo album, I finished my first cup of joe quickly. No big deal, though. I buy my k-cups in bulk, so I'm always prepared to pump up my caffeine levels. Before I had a chance to brew my second cup of the day, my phone rang. It was Lisa.

"Hello," I answered reluctantly.

"So, are you still mad at me?"

"I'm not mad at you." I lied to her, but it was easier than telling her how I really felt.

"Aww....I'm so glad to hear that! I was worried about you, so I called out sick to spend the day with you. I want you to tell me everything that's going on, and I promise to be a good listener! Sound good?"

"That sounds great, Lisa. It will have to wait until this afternoon, though. I have an appointment this morning."

"Another appointment? What's going on with you? Are you keeping something from me?"

"I'll explain later, ok? Meet me here at, say 1:00. I'll pick up a pizza, and we can have lunch and talk."

"Ok, that will give me time to get beautiful."

"You don't need any time for that. You're always beautiful."

"Aww, thanks Baby! Flattery will get you everywhere!" She giggled, and we said our goodbyes.

Something is up with her. She's being too nice. Maybe I'm the one who should be concerned. It's starting to feel like *she* is keeping something from *me*.

Oh well, there's no time to worry about that right now. I added cream and sugar to my coffee, and returned to the photo album on my kitchen table. The album contained some photos of individuals I couldn't identify. Page after page, my search continued. Most of the photos were black and white, but a few of the more recent shots were in color. Pictures of mom and dad, Charlie, Aunt Peg, and even one of me in my Cub Scout uniform were all in color. As I reached the last page of the album, once again I saw the photo of Caleb. I hadn't noticed this before, but he appeared to be at a picnic, with several other people in the background. Wait a minute....wait just a minute! I ran to my junk drawer and dug through its contents. Toward the back of the drawer, I found what I was looking for. I grabbed my magnifying glass and went back to the kitchen table. Holding it close to the photo of Caleb, everything became much clearer. Standing behind, and slightly to the right of Caleb, was a woman. And there was no denying the woman I was looking at was definitely the same woman who was in my dream. But who is she? Or should I say, who *was* she?

Caleb and Flora were the same age, more or less. The

woman in the photo is definitely younger than Caleb. If I had to guess, I'd say Caleb was roughly 50 in this photo, and this woman was maybe 30. So, it certainly wasn't Flora. Oh well, another mystery that will never be solved. No time to worry about it right now, though. I have to be on time for my appointment.

Changing into a pair of jeans and a black polo shirt, I was ready. Boy, was I ready!

I was nervous, but hoping to connect with someone…anyone! Hopefully, Tina will give me some answers. Time will tell.

Chapter 15

I arrived at Tina's office with a few minutes to spare. From the exterior, it didn't look like much. It was an old house, in terrible shape, and it definitely needed a coat of paint. When I walked through the front door, I was pleasantly surprised. The interior was actually very nice. Fresh paint, refinished hardwood floors, and a staircase with varnished railings made the inside look great. I kept thinking that maybe the owner should concentrate more on the outside appearance. The house had been divided up into 4 offices. Tina's was on the 2nd floor, in the back of the building. At the top of the stairs, Tina's office door was on the left. The sign on the door read 'Tina White, LLC' I didn't know a single person could be an LLC. But maybe she's not a single person. Maybe she has an entire team of mediums working with her? Oh well, it doesn't matter. Just as long as she can help me.

As I knocked on the door, a voice came from the other side. "Come on in….it's open!"

Pushing the door open, I walked into a large, rectangular shaped room. The walls were painted a light peach, and there was a beige carpet on the floor. A desk, a file cabinet, and several office chairs were on the right side of the room. On the left was a sofa, recliner, coffee table, and a few large houseplants. Next to the sofa was the bathroom door. The door was closed, but water was definitely running in the sink.

The same voice came from the bathroom."Is that you, Jason?"

"Yes, it's me. Am I too early?"

"Nope, not at all. I'm just making coffee. Have a seat, and I'll be right with you."

The couch and recliner both looked super comfortable, but I decided on an office chair instead.

After taking a seat, the bathroom door opened and out stepped one of the most beautiful women I've ever seen. Long brunette hair, hazel eyes, high cheekbones, and a cute little pointed nose. Not one drop of makeup was on her face. She didn't need it. She was wearing jeans and a hoodie, with running shoes on her feet. Nothing fancy....but she would look good regardless of what she was wearing.

"Hi Jason, I'm Tina White. It's so nice to meet you!"

I stood to shake hands with her. "Likewise Tina. Thank you so much for seeing me today!"

"You're very welcome! Hopefully, I can be of some help to you."

"Dr. Phillips recommended you," I commented. "He said you helped him a great deal."

"Ken's a great guy. I'm so happy we could make contact with his mother."

Tina poured two cups of coffee. "Cream and sugar?" she asked.

"Yes, please."

I took my seat again, and she sat in the office chair next to me. I'm glad she didn't sit behind her desk. It would have felt like sitting in the principal's office in high school.

"So, have you ever had a reading?"

"Excuse me?"

"A reading....have you ever seen a medium before?"

"Oh, I'm sorry." Boy, did I feel like a jerk. "No, this is my first time."

"So normally, for a new client, I would do a reading and try to make contact. But, since you have more than one spirit you want to connect with, I'd like to hear your story first."

"Really?" I asked.

"Yeah, absolutely. Start at the very beginning and tell me everything that's been happening in your life. If you don't mind, I'm going to take some notes."

"No, not at all." I was happy that someone was interested in listening to me.

"Cool. Let me know when you're ready for a refill on your coffee."

So, I did what she asked me to do. I started at the very beginning, telling her everything about my family, my job, my life, Lisa, and all the crazy dreams and visions that had been driving me crazy. I explained I had physically seen Caleb, Vince, and the crying women. I told her of my visit to Dr. Phillips, and his suggestion that a medium would be more helpful to me than an increase in medication.

Tina interrupted me. "Wait a minute. I'm a little confused. You say you've already seen spirits. So why do you feel you need to see a medium?"

"I've *seen* them, but only *heard* a few words. We haven't been able to do much communicating."

Tina replied, "Ahh....so you are clairvoyant. In other words, you can *see* spirits. I can see them also, but my real strength is clairaudience, or the ability to *hear* spirits."

"So you and I might make a pretty good team?"

"Maybe, you never know."

I glanced down at my watch and saw the time. Damn it! 3:00 already...where did the time go? Lisa will be pissed at me. It was then that I remembered leaving my phone in the car. I didn't want to take any chances of being disturbed. I can just imagine the texts and voicemails I have.

"Tina, I am so sorry. I have to cut this short. I didn't realize how late it was. Can we continue this another time?"

"Absolutely, and there's no need to apologize. I have a date this evening, so I need to get going too."

What a lucky guy. I'd give anything to be in his shoes. Maybe it was Dr. Phillips...he never disclosed what type of relationship they had. Oh well, I have enough problems with the relationship I'm in. I definitely don't need any more headaches.

Tina checked the calendar on her phone and said, "I'm going to be pretty busy tomorrow, but Thursday looks good. Ten o'clock again?"

"Sounds good! I'll see you then."

Chapter 16

I checked my phone before I left Tina's parking lot. 16 Text messages, 8 Voicemails, and 3 emails....all from Lisa. Oh boy, this would not be an enjoyable evening. I didn't bother checking any of the messages. I pretty much knew what to expect.

As I drove home, I couldn't stop thinking about Tina. Her beauty and her sweet personality made it so easy to talk with her. She made me feel important, listening to every word and every thought I had. Thursday couldn't come soon enough. Tina exudes a sense of confidence, yet she is not overly self-assured. I have faith that she will be able to connect with the spirits that can help me.

Pulling into my driveway, I was surprised to see Lisa's car and Kyle's pickup truck. It was odd that both of them were there. Lisa and Kyle never liked each other, so I tried to keep them far apart. It was easier and safer that way. Before I could get my car door open, they both came running out of my apartment with concerned looks on their faces.

"Where have you been?" cried Lisa. "I've been worried sick! You didn't respond to me, so I called Kyle." Lisa wrapped her arms around me and squeezed tightly. So, she wasn't mad after all. That was a pleasant surprise.

After Lisa let go, Kyle gave me a hug, and asked if everything was ok.

"Things are getting better. Thanks for being patient with me, buddy. I should be back at work soon."

"Take your time, Jay. There's no rush....come back when

you're ready, ok?"

"Yep, thanks again." Something was wrong, though. Something was very wrong. Lisa and Kyle have a mutual hatred toward each other, yet here they were, together in my apartment. And when Kyle hugged me, I didn't smell his usual cologne. He had the overwhelming odor of Lisa's perfume. The perfume I gave her last Christmas.

Lisa and I said goodbye to Kyle as he drove away.. Holding hands, we started walking towards my apartment door. After only taking a few steps, I stopped and turned towards Lisa.

"Care to tell me why your perfume scent is all over Kyle?"

"Excuse me? What are you talking about?"

"When Kyle hugged me, I could smell your perfume. He smelled like he took a bath in it."

"Are you serious? Jay, I've been so upset, not knowing where you were. And all you can do is accuse me of cheating on you with your best friend!"

"First, I was only 2 hours late. There was no need to call out the National Guard. Second, you know I haven't been working, and you supposedly don't even like Kyle, so why would you call *him*? And finally, I haven't accused you of anything. You're the one who mentioned cheating!"

Lisa glanced down at the ground and pulled her hand away. She looked up, and her eyes met mine.

"Jay, what is happening to us? Things used to be so good, but lately we can't seem to get along."

"Now you know the reason I don't want to set a wedding date. Things wouldn't be any better for us if we were married."

"So, are you saying that you don't want to marry me?"

Answering her was one of the hardest things I've ever had to do. "I don't know what I'm saying, Lisa. Can you give me some time to get my shit together?"

Lisa looked at me impatiently. "Just don't take too long. I'm not getting any younger," she said with a smile on her face.

Since we hadn't eaten lunch yet, we decided to walk to the Ventura Diner. It was just a short walk, and the weather was beautiful. The Diner had been in business for at least 50 years, going through several owners and at least a half dozen remodels in that time. The current owners were Greek, but the menu is the same as it has always been, and the food is actually tastier than in the past. We arrived at The Diner at 4:30, just narrowly beating the dinner rush. When we entered, the owner (I think his name is Nico) was running to answer the phone. He told us to sit wherever we wanted and Gloria would be right with us.

The interior of The Diner featured an aqua color scheme, with chrome trim moldings and LED lights around the ceiling line. It sounds gaudy, but it's actually quite attractive. We took a seat in the last booth on the right, near the bathrooms. Gloria Ferguson was our waitress. She has fiery red hair, and a pretty good body for a woman in her late 40s. Her uniforms are tight and low cut, and definitely help her get bigger tips than any of the other waitresses there.

"Hi guys!" Gloria greeted us with a smile. "You need menus, or do you know what you're having?"

Lisa ordered for both of us, "Two cheeseburger deluxes, with sweet potato fries, and 2 large cokes, please."

"You got it, hon! Food should be out in a few minutes." Gloria moved on to the next table.

Lisa reached across the table and grabbed my hand. "I told you that I would be a good listener, and I meant it. So, please tell me what's going on with you, Jay. I really want to understand."

"Lisa, it's not easy to describe what I've been going through. It's like the past and the present are fighting over...."

As I gazed up the center aisle of the diner, something caught my attention near the cashier. Standing and staring back at me was the crying woman in my dream. The same woman in my photo album. Still dressed in black, with tears streaming down her cheeks, she was speaking to me. But not with audible words. The words that she spoke, and there weren't many of them, could only be heard in my mind.

"I'm sorry, I'm so sorry!" repeated over and over in my head.

I felt bad for her. I hate to see anyone cry, but she obviously felt she had done something hurtful to me. Slowly standing and moving towards her, I smiled, hoping to reassure her she had caused no pain.

"Don't cry, please don't cry!" I spoke to her and held out my hand, but almost instantly she disappeared. I was so close, almost able to reach out and touch her. Now I had a dozen employees and customers of the Ventura Diner staring at me, thinking that I had lost it. I could just imagine their thoughts. Maybe I am losing it.

I smiled at all the curious faces, apologized, and turned to return to my seat. As I did, Lisa stood and walked towards me.

"Come on, we're getting out of here," she hissed.

"But we haven't eaten yet."

"I don't care, we're leaving." She threw some money at the cashier on the way out, and dragged me down the stairs, out to the parking lot. "What the hell is wrong with you?? I have never been so embarrassed in my entire life!"

We walked back to my apartment without speaking. Her social status was more important than trying to communicate with her fiancé. All of her talk about wanting to lend an ear was just talk.

When we returned to the parking area for my car, I unlocked it and got in.

"Where are you going?" shouted Lisa.

"Out for dinner. I'm hungry, and you wouldn't let me eat my cheeseburger."

"Jay, wait! Can't we talk? I don't understand what just happened."

"I don't understand it myself," I answered abruptly. "I've tried talking with you, and it's not working. When I figure it out, I'll let you know."

I closed the door of my PT Cruiser and pulled away. I couldn't take any more. I needed food and answers. I'll get some food tonight, and hopefully some answers on Thursday.

Chapter 17

I woke up early Wednesday morning, with indigestion from the fast food I'd eaten the night before. Burgers made from 50% lean meat, and 50% preservatives really did a job on my gut. When will I learn I can't eat that junk? Oh well, 10 or 12 Tums should help me make it through the morning.

I sat down at the kitchen table with my first cup of coffee of the day. The clock on my stove said 6:05am. Damn, why can't I get a good night's sleep? Maybe I need to take some sleeping pills. Maybe I just need to bite the bullet and marry Lisa. Sure, we could have a few kids. She could be the mayor of Ventura, and I could be a stay at home dad. Life would be so grand! I took a big gulp of coffee and almost choked on it. What the hell is wrong with me? I don't want to be a stay at home dad. Honestly, I don't want to be a dad....at least not yet. And I don't want to marry Lisa.

It took a long time to come to that realization, but I just felt a 115 lb weight lifted off my shoulders. Sure, Lisa is beautiful and sexy, but that's where the attraction ends. She is also selfish, spoiled, noncommunicative, and she can also be thoughtless and disrespectful. Maybe it's time to end our relationship and get on with our lives. Now, I just have to get the balls to tell her.

Anyway, on with today's project. If the visions of Caleb's murder are true, then there should be something in his autopsy to confirm this. In other words, if the coroner felt Caleb died of a heart attack, but his face and skull were brutally shattered, then that should throw up a red flag. Even if his head hit the steering wheel when his truck landed in Lake Menderville, it shouldn't have done too much damage to his face. But, here's my problem...autopsy reports aren't posted on Ancestry's website. So, I would have to go to the Crandall County Medical Examiner's Office in Aaron and put in a request for a copy of the autopsy. That's assuming they even keep records for 70 years. I don't want to waste a lot of time searching for an autopsy record that may have been destroyed a long time ago. There is one person who might be able to help me. Sue Horton is an old high school sweetheart of mine. Well, not really a sweetheart, so to speak. We were good friends throughout high school, but during our senior year, we tried to take it to the next level. I asked her out on a date...a proper date. We went out to dinner, and to the drive-in movies. The movie was boring, and gave us the opportunity to kiss a few times, but it just didn't feel right. It was kind of like kissing your sister, or so I've been told. (I never had a sister.) At the end of the evening, we both agreed that we were better off as good friends. Anyway, Sue Horton is now the county clerk of Crandall County. If anyone could help me, it would definitely be her.

I found Sue's number on the Crandall County website and dialed it. She answered after just one ring.

"County Clerk's office, Sue speaking, how may I help you?"

"Hey babe, how about going to the drive-in movies with me tonight?"

Sue laughed. "Didn't we try that about 15 years ago?"

I chuckled, "Well, it didn't work the first time, so maybe we could try it again?"

"Yeah right. Look, I'm pretty busy, so do you need something, or did you just call to be a pain in the ass?"

"Sorry Sue. I need to know how long the medical examiner's office holds on to autopsy reports."

"Why ask me? You know that's not my department!" Sue was confused.

"I know. It's just an odd request and I don't know who I should speak with."

"Marge Wilson takes care of all the medical examiner's records. She'd be the person to talk to. Hold on and I'll transfer you, ok?"

"Wait, Sue!" I yelled into the phone. "The autopsy I'm interested in took place 70 years ago."

There was a long pause, and finally Sue replied, "Are you serious? Why would you need a 70-year-old autopsy report?" She was skeptical, and I can't say that I blame her.

"It's hard to explain, but do you remember back in high school, I told you about my great-grandfather drowning in Lake Menderville?"

"You mean the man who drove his truck into the lake?" asked Sue.

"Yeah, that's the one. Well, I came across some evidence that suggests there may have been some foul play involved."

There was another unsettling pause before Sue said, "What kind of evidence? Shouldn't you report it to the police and let them handle it?"

I didn't want her to think I'm a complete idiot, so I responded with a rational reply. "I can't divulge the source of the evidence just yet, and I'd like to have a little more to present to the authorities."

Sue was still perplexed when she replied, "So why don't you want to speak with Marge?"

I replied, "Because you carry a lot of clout. If a 70-year-old document still exists, you would get better results than I would."

"Oh my God, you're such a brown noser! Give me a day or two, and I'll see what I can come up with, okay?"

I thanked Sue and said goodbye, knowing that she would do everything in her power to help me.

Chapter 18

Thursday morning finally arrived, and I was super excited to see Tina again. I had a strange feeling that this was going to be the day that I would receive some communication from my family. When I knocked on her office door, I felt a moment of disappointment when there was no answer. After waiting a few seconds, I knocked again, but there was still no response. Feeling dejected, I turned and headed for the stairs. Suddenly, the front door slammed shut, and Tina came running up the staircase.

"Oh my God, Jason, I'm so sorry I'm late. It's been one of those mornings where everything has gone wrong!"

When she made it to the top of the staircase, our eyes met, and I froze. Today, Tina was wearing an aqua colored silk blouse, black skirt, stockings, and heels. She was also wearing makeup, not much, but just enough to enhance her features, and a gold necklace and bracelet.

I was speechless. She was beautiful the last time we met....today she's drop-dead gorgeous.

"What's wrong?" she asked. "Are you mad because I'm late?"

"M-mad? No, no, not at all." I could feel my heart racing in my chest. "What makes you think I'm mad?"

"Well, honestly, it's the way you're staring at me."

Since she's a psychic, she probably knew what I was thinking anyway, so I let it fly. "I'm staring at you because you look great!"

Tina smiled and thanked me. "That's so nice of you to say! Well, should we go in and get started?"

She didn't slap me, so I guess that was a good sign.

Tina unlocked her office door, opened it, and turned the office lights on.

"Come on in....you want coffee?"

I smiled and said, "Does a bear shit in the woods?"

"Excuse me?"

Apparently, that expression wasn't familiar to her. "Never mind." Boy, did I feel like an ass.

While Tina was making coffee, she asked if there had been any more spiritual visits. I told her about seeing *and* hearing the crying woman at the diner. Again, I reiterated that there was very little verbal communication. In addition, I shared my thoughts on Caleb and what an autopsy report might reveal.

She thought about it for a moment and chimed in, "Interesting idea, but I think it's likely a long shot. As for this crying woman, any idea who that might be?"

"No, but she's in a photo with Caleb, so I'm assuming she's either family, or a close friend of Caleb and Flora."

As we drank our coffee, I decided to be nosey. "Did you have a good time on your date?"

Tina rolled her eyes and chuckled. "It was, in fact, one of the worst dates I've ever been on."

"Oh, I'm so sorry," I said. Actually, I was thrilled that she was still available.

"Don't be sorry, Jason. I'm still getting over a terrible relationship, and break-up. That's what led me to seek help from Dr. Phillips. So, I'm very cautious about letting someone new in to my life. When the right guy comes along, I'll know it. But enough about me. What do you say we get started?"

"Sounds good," I replied. So that's why she sees Dr. Phillips. She's definitely not a whacko.

We sat in the office chairs, facing each other. The lighting in her office was low and relaxing. Tina clasped her hands and lowered her head. I assumed she was praying, but wasn't sure, so I just kept quiet. After about 30 seconds, she raised her head, but kept her eyes shut. We sat this way for a long time. At least it felt like a long time. Finally, Tina shook her head and spoke. "I'm not getting anything." She reached out to me, and said, "Take my hands, and pray with me."

I did as she said, but told her I haven't prayed in a long time.

"That's okay. Close your eyes and concentrate on the words I'm about to speak."

"Okay, whatever you say." I closed my eyes tightly and listened for Tina's voice.

She spoke softly, "Heavenly Father, Jason and I come to you today to thank you and ask for your help. We wish to connect with Jason's ancestors, so we ask that you allow his spirit guides to bring members of his family to us, and allow us to communicate with them. We thank you and worship you, Lord. Amen."

I started to speak, but Tina shushed me.

After about 5 minutes of silence, she opened her eyes and spoke. "You said Caleb was a farmer, right?"

"Yep."

Tina had an unclear look on her face when she said, "Do you have a map of Caleb's property?"

"No, I don't even know where his property was."

"Okay, he's telling me to look at a map."

"You saw him? You really saw him? And he spoke to you? So, I'm not crazy after all!" Darn, I wish I could have seen what Tina saw.

"Yes, silly, he's standing right behind you."

I turned to look, but told her I saw nothing.

"Who's the medium here, me or you?"

"You are."

"Then shut up and let me earn my money!"

I lowered my head and apologized, but Tina assured me there's no need for apologies.

Neither of us understood what was happening, but I asked anyway, "What map is Caleb speaking of?"

"Darn it, he's gone. He didn't say what map, just 'Look at the map.' That's all I got."

I got out my phone and started searching.

"What are you doing?" asked Tina.

"Well, Caleb died back in 1952, so we would have to look at a map made before his death."

"Ahh, I get where you're going. But historical maps probably will not show the names of property owners."

"You're right. I didn't think of that."

"How about old tax maps?" asked Tina.

"Yep, and I know where we can get them! My friend Sue is the County Clerk of Crandall County. She's trying to find a copy of Caleb's autopsy. It's too late to bother her today, but maybe if I bribe her with a coffee and some donuts tomorrow morning, she can come up with the map we need."

Tina smiled at me. "Cool! Mind if I tag along?"

"Are you kidding? That would be awesome! I'll pick you up at 9:00am tomorrow. Is that okay?"

"Yep, it's a date!"

I think I died and went to heaven.

Chapter 19

After stopping for some Chinese food on my way home from Tina's, the sun had set, and it was getting dark outside. Upon entering my apartment, I felt a familiar presence.

"Hello Jason."

I recognized the voice before turning my apartment lights on. It was a whispery voice that was not audible to the ear, yet I could hear it in my mind. "Vince, is that you?"

"Yes sir, it's me."

"Well, hello again. But this time, you're not turning out the lights, and you're not going to show me strange visions of my family. I have questions, and I need some answers. Okay?"

"Sure thing! Ask away."

"First off, I need to turn the lights on so I can see where the hell I'm going. Is that okay with you?"

"Absolutely, whatever you like!"

After a quick flip of the switch, my apartment was lit, and before me stood a shadowy, outlined figure I recognized as Vince.

"So, what is it you want from me?" I asked.

"Don't be afraid of me, Jason. I just want to help you."

"Help me how? What are you trying to show me?"

"Your life could be in danger. I just want you to be safe."

Vince wasn't making any sense, but at least I could communicate with him.

"So, are you what's known as a spirit guide?" I questioned him.

"I'm *your* spirit guide," said Vince.

His reply sent chills to my bones. "So, you were at Tina's office today?"

"I was."

"And how is my life in danger?"

"I must go now, Jason. Remain cautious, and I will be there for you."

"Wait Vince, I have more questions...." But he was gone.

I sat at my kitchen table for a few moments, trying to absorb everything that had happened to me in the past week. It wasn't long ago that I felt so alone in this world. Now I have family members trying to contact me from the spirit world, I met my spirit guide, and a gorgeous medium is trying to help me make sense of all of this. At least my life isn't boring.

I was ready to go to bed when there was a knock at the door. Who could this be? Another family member? It would be awesome if it was Tina! No, she doesn't know where I live. Slowly, I stepped toward the door. As I opened it, Lisa stuck her nose in.

"Hey, can I talk with you?" Lisa slurred her words. Obviously, she had been drinking.

"Sure, come on in." There were some things I needed to say, but in her condition, she might not remember them tomorrow.

She was unsteady on her feet as she entered my apartment. Pulling close, she gave me a big hug and a sloppy, wet kiss.

"I hope you're not driving," I remarked.

"What difference does it make? Daddy's the mayor....I won't get a DWI," she laughed.

"Not funny, Lisa." She didn't drink often, but when she did, she was obnoxious and rude.

"Soooorrrryyy! You don't have to be so touchy!"

"I'm not being touchy. I'm just concerned about your safety and the safety of other people on the roads."

She grabbed me and tried to kiss me again as I pulled away. "Then I'll just have to spend the night," she said, with a wink of her eye.

"Lisa, I can smell three distinct odors on you. Booze, cigarettes, and Kyle's cologne. I'm not particularly fond of any of them." The look on her face was all the proof I needed. She had just got caught with her hand in the cookie jar.

"Look, Kyle and I are just friends. I called him because I was worried about you."

Perhaps laughing in her face wasn't the right thing to do, but I can tell a lie when I hear it. And this was definitely a lie. "I'm calling a cab for you. You can't stay here tonight, and you're in no shape to drive."

"But what about my car?" Lisa asked.

"Call your boyfriend, Kyle. Maybe he'll come get it."

I stood outside with Lisa and waited for the taxi to arrive. The strange thing about all of this was, I didn't feel sad, hurt, or angry. Quite the contrary, I felt relieved and relaxed.

"You know I love you, right Jay?" Tears covered her face.

"Lisa, I don't believe you know what love is."

"And there's nothing going on between me and Kyle," Lisa insisted.

"I don't believe you." She began sobbing louder. "Stop your blubbering, Lisa. Isn't this what you want? I'm giving you my blessing. I want to be happy, and I want you to be happy. Go to Kyle, and live a happy life, ok?"

"I can't. You and I must have kids together."

"We *must* have? Why *must* we have kids together?"

Lisa was crying uncontrollably at this point. "Because Daddy said....I mean because I love you!"

I didn't like where this was going. "Daddy said what? Lisa, what did Daddy say?"

Just then, the cab showed up. Lisa ran and jumped into the back seat. I gave the driver a twenty and told him Lisa's address. Lisa was still crying as she sat in the back of the cab.

"I'll get your things together and drop them off to you."

The driver pulled away, and I prayed he was taking at least some of my problems with him.

Chapter 20

Friday morning, the weather was outstanding! Plenty of sunshine, and a light breeze blowing, had the makings for a perfect day. The fifteen minute drive from Ventura to Aaron was awesome. With my PT Cruiser's sunroof open, and George Jones playing on the stereo, it was like a dream come true. I went to the drive-thru lane of Aaron Donuts and ordered three coffees and a dozen assorted donuts. Tina's office was just a hop, skip, and jump away, so I would be there right at 9:00am.

When I pulled into Tina's parking lot, a familiar pickup truck was leaving. It was Kyle! Apparently, he didn't notice me as he pulled out. Immediately, my heart sank to the pit of my stomach. I could feel a rush of anxiety, which completely overwhelmed me. Why was Kyle here? What was he doing here? Was he here to visit Tina? No, not today....I can't deal with this today.

I parked my car, closed my eyes, and focused on my breathing. I took deep breaths and slowly started counting backwards from 100. It took several minutes for my heart to stop racing.

I had just dealt with the knowledge of Kyle having an affair with my fiancé. Although Tina and I had just met, I felt a strange connection to her, and had hopes of our friendship growing. I didn't need Kyle spoiling that, too. He and I had been best friends for a long time. But now I wondered if he had ever been a loyal friend, or did he just keep me around so I wouldn't suspect him of sleeping with Lisa?

Suddenly, a car pulled into the lot and parked next to mine. It was Tina. As she got out of her car, she smiled and waved to me.

"I'm so sorry, I'm late again. Have you been waiting long?"

"No, just a few minutes. I got you a coffee....cream and sugar, right?"

"Yes, thank you so much! I have a lot to tell you. My spirit guide connected with me this morning, and tried to give me warnings about your safety and mine. The messages weren't very clear, though. Maybe we can talk later and try to connect again?"

"That sounds great, Tina. Before we go over to the courthouse, I need to ask you a question." I didn't want to come on too headstrong, but I really needed to know.

"Okay, ask away."

"Do you know of a man? Muscular, with long hair, drives a big brown Ford pickup truck?"

"Unfortunately, yes I do. Kyle's the jerk I went out with earlier this week. I told him we're not compatible, but he won't leave me alone. Do you know him?"

I smiled and felt so relieved. "Yeah, that's my ex-boss and my ex-best friend. He's also having an affair with my ex-fiancé. He was leaving here when I arrived."

"Oh my God, Jason, I'm so sorry. So, it's officially over between you and Lisa?"

"Yes, but please don't be sorry. I'm not. In fact, I feel great!"

"Good for you, I'm glad!" she said warmly. "I mean, I'm glad you're ok. Not glad that Lisa cheated on you."

What a woman. Besides being gorgeous, she was genuinely a super nice person....the kind of person I could sit and talk with for hours.

"So, if he's having an affair with Lisa, why is he bothering me?"

"I don't know for sure. Lisa showed up at my apartment last night, drunk off her ass. Maybe she's developing a drinking problem, and Kyle doesn't like it?"

"Could be. So, did Lisa spend the night with you?" Tina asked shyly.

Did I just hear that correctly? Did I detect a bit of jealousy? No one has ever been jealous of me in my entire life! I needed to slow down....maybe I'm reading into this too much.

"No, I called a cab and sent her home."

Tina gave me a 'thumbs up' and said, "Good job!"

"Well, we should get going. Would you like to ride in *Petey*?" I asked.

"Petey?" She looked confused.

"Yes, *Petey Cruiser*." I pointed to my car.

Tina looked at me inquisitively. "You named your car?"

I nodded.

"That's cute....but we'll take my car."

*   *   *

It was only a ten-minute drive to the County Courthouse. Sitting on top of a grassy knoll with well-kept sidewalks and a large parking lot, the courthouse was awe-inspiring. A beautiful, Romanesque Revival building in excellent condition, it was more than just a courthouse. Inside, there were offices for every department of Crandall County, from Sheriff to Animal Control to Coroner, and everything in between.

Tina parked her Nissan Rogue, we grabbed our coffee and donuts, and walked to the entrance. The lobby of the four-story building had a large department directory hanging on the wall to the left. Beautiful marble floors, an attractive shade of beige paint on the walls, and antique lighting fixtures on the ceiling added to the ambience of the building. Sue was the County Clerk. Her office was on the first floor, directly ahead of us. With three people working under her, I knew she had worked her butt off to climb up the ladder so quickly. Her ex-husband, Bob, was the Highway Dept. Supervisor.

We walked through the open door into Sue's office, and announced that we've come bearing gifts. Sue greeted us with a smile and jokingly told us to leave the food on the counter and get out. Sue was always a ball-buster throughout high school, so I never took her seriously.

She stepped around the counter and gave me a hug and a peck on the cheek. Although she was a few pounds heavier than in high school, Sue still looked great.

"How are you, Jay? Long time, no see."

"I'm good, Sue! It's nice to see you."

Sue looked at Tina and said, "Are you with him? God, I feel sorry for you."

Tina laughed and introduced herself.

"It's very nice to meet you," said Sue, as they shook hands. Then she turned to me and said, "And as for you, I have good news and bad news. The Crandall County Coroner, in 1952, was Stan Robbins. Stan was a hoarder. He saved all of his paperwork....25 years worth of it! All of his records were put into file boxes, and the boxes were stored in a large room up on the fourth floor. Stan retired in 1975, and as far as we know, all of his files are still upstairs. That's the good news. Now for the bad news. No one ever labeled those boxes with their contents."

Tina was just as excited as I was. "That shouldn't be a problem. How many boxes could there be?"

"Marge estimated that there were approximately 250 boxes, and there are also boxes of DPW and Animal Control records mixed in."

"Oh boy," I said. "How long is it going to take Marge to go through all those boxes?"

"Marge isn't going through any boxes. She's overloaded with work as it is. She just doesn't have the time."

"So what do we do?" I asked.

"*We* don't do anything," Sue replied. "Take the elevator to the fourth floor, go to the end of the hallway, and through the double doors. We close at four, so make sure you're out before then, otherwise you'll get locked in for the night."

I tried my hardest to look daggers at Sue, but it didn't work. She just laughed at me.

"Oh, one more thing. I need a 1950 property tax map of

Ventura."

"I'm not even going to ask why. It shouldn't be a problem, though. I have most of those maps saved on the computer. Anything in particular you're looking for?" asked Sue.

"Yes. Any and all property owned by Caleb Thompson."

"Is he the guy that drowned back in the 50s?"

"Yep, that's him."

"Okay, why don't you go upstairs and start searching? Tina can hang out with me while I find your map, and I'll send her up when we're finished."

I told the girls that I'd be back in a few weeks and made my way to the fourth floor.

Chapter 21

T hings were pretty quiet up on the fourth floor. Lights were on in the hallway, but other than that, there wasn't much going on. Many large meeting rooms that didn't get used very often occupied the fourth floor. At the end of the corridor was the room I was looking for. I opened the doors and placed doorstops so they wouldn't slam shut on me. Even in the darkness, I could see the stacks of cardboard file boxes. The sunlight was blocked from entering the room because they were stacked in front of the windows. I could already tell that this was going to take a long time. Maybe it was a waste of time. Would the autopsy report be of any help? I had to at least try.

As I searched for the light switch, a whispering voice called out my name. Unsure if it was just my imagination, I continued to feel my way through the dark, searching for the elusive switch. The voice called me a second time, and this time there was no denying it.

"Jason." The voice was very clear.

I turned to listen, but the voice became silent. Across the room from where I was standing, a blinding beam of light shone through the mountain of boxes stacked in front of the windows. The light was aimed at a single box, lying alone on the floor in the center of the room. It doesn't take a rocket scientist to understand that a beam of light can not permeate a mountain of cardboard boxes filled with files and folders. So, I cautiously approached the lone box. The stench of mildew and rotting paper slapped me in the face when I removed the box cover. I reached in and grabbed a folder that was protruding from the other folders in the box. To my amazement, my search was over! 'Caleb Thompson-Autopsy Performed June 14, 1952' was written on the outside of the folder. This was not luck, and I couldn't even consider it fate. It was more of a *spiritual intervention*. If I had to guess, I'd say that Vince was involved in some way.

To lead me to the exact box, and the exact folder I was looking for, was mind-blowing. Explaining this to Sue would not be easy.

After putting the lid back on the box, I grabbed my folder, and the beam of light disappeared. It seems that Vince is a master of using light and darkness. I closed the double doors and jogged to the elevator. I was eager to see if Sue was able to locate the tax map from 1950.

"Did you forget something, Jay?" Tina asked as I returned to Sue's office.

I didn't know what to say. I just smiled and shook my head. Tina and Sue both looked at me curiously.

Sue grinned and said, "Let me guess, you had an uncontrollable craving for another donut?"

"Nope, I found what I need," I replied as I held up the folder.

"Get the hell out of here!" said Sue. "You were only up there for 5 minutes. How'd you manage that one?"

"I don't know....just lucky, I guess. Can I make copies of these papers?"

Sue assured me I didn't need to make copies. "Those papers should have been shredded years ago. You can keep them."

I thanked her and asked how she was making out with the map I had asked for.

"Really!? You don't give a girl a chance. You've only been gone for five minutes!"

"Sorry Sue. I'm just anxious to get some answers."

"Okay, let's see what we have here," Sue said as she gazed into the pc monitor. "In 1950, Caleb Thompson owned a rather large tract of land off of Roberts Road. That would be right here." She pointed to the spot on the map she was referring to. "Looks like about 90 acres. His house and barns were on said property. And he also owned an additional 30 acres adjacent to the 90 acre lot. You can see it right here," she pointed to another spot on the screen. That lot is off of Browns Road, but if I remember right, there is a heavy outcropping of bedrock, which would make it impossible to access that by car.

"Anything else?" I asked.

"Nope."

Sue printed a copy of the map and handed it to me. "That'll be $250 please."

"Okay, put it on my tab." I gave Sue a hug and thanked her again.

"Nice meeting you, Sue," said Tina as we left the courthouse.

When we got in Tina's car, I thanked her for accompanying me today.

"But I didn't do anything," she replied.

"You were there for moral support, and that's important to me."

Tina smiled at me, and said, "Sue told me what a great guy you are. She thinks that we're together….you know, as a couple."

Our eyes met briefly, and I could feel the warmth of her heart. Oh well, I need to keep focused.

"Did you tell her we're not?"

"No."

I left it at that. When we returned to Tina's office, she told me she had two hours to kill before her next appointment.

"Let's go up to my office. I'll make some coffee, and we can talk."

"Sounds good!" I grabbed my papers and followed her inside.

As Tina made the coffee, I opened the file on Caleb. Caleb was 57 when he died, with no known ailments. The autopsy report listed every broken bone in his skull, most of which I couldn't even pronounce. I didn't even know there were that many bones in the skull. Several front teeth were broken and/ or missing. No sign of myocardial infarction or cerebrovascular disease. In other words, he didn't die of a heart attack or stroke.

No water found in the lungs. I got out my phone and did a Google search.

"Find anything?" Tina asked, as she handed me a cup of coffee and sat in the chair next to me.

I found what I was looking for on my phone. "Did you know that if a person were to die, and then fall into the water, no water would enter their lungs?"

"Really? Why is that?"

"Because there's air in the lungs, which prevents water from entering. And because the person has stopped breathing, this air remains and continues to keep the water out."

"I assume there was no water found in Caleb's lungs?" asked Tina.

"Nope. No water, but yet the coroner listed 'drowning' as the cause of death. No heart attack, no stroke, and nearly every bone in the front of his skull was broken."

"Oh my God! Poor Caleb must have died a very violent death!" Tina was visibly upset.

"No doubt. I don't understand why the coroner declared that drowning was the cause of death."

"Sounds like a cover-up to me."

"You know, I'm really glad you said that. I was thinking the same thing, but if I had said it, I'd be labeled a conspiracy theorist."

"Jay, I don't mean to change the subject, but how did you find the autopsy report so quickly?"

"I almost forgot.... I met my spirit guide! It's Vince. Vince is my spirit guide, and he led me to the box that held the autopsy report!"

"Oh my God, that is so exciting! I'm so happy for you!"

"That reminds me, you said you had connected with your spirit guide?"

"I did. Unfortunately, I don't have time to talk about it right now. I have a reading in thirty minutes, and I need to get ready."

"Okay, no problem." I didn't want this day to end. "Maybe we could get together this evening?" I asked nervously.

"I'm sorry Jay, but I have a date tonight."

Ouch! I didn't see that one coming. Honestly, it felt like we were making a connection. I guess I was wrong. Maybe it's for the best....I need to stay focused, and try to figure out the meaning of all the dreams and visions I've been having. "You're not going out with Kyle again, are you?" I asked.

Tina laughed and said, "Oh God, no! Never! I'm going out with a guy I used to date back in high school."

I told Tina to have fun on her date and hurriedly left her office. I didn't want the disappointment on my face to show.

Chapter 22

I awoke, soaked in sweat, with my heart beating wildly, and my head pounding with the worst headache I've ever had. It was Saturday morning, 7:00am, and my cell phone was already ringing. Jumping up off the couch, I grabbed my phone from the coffee table. It was Tina.

"Hello?" My voice was gravelly from waking with a parched mouth.

"Jay, I'm sorry to wake you so early, but I need to speak with you. Would it be okay if I came to your place?"

Of course I said yes. Who wouldn't? I texted her my address, did some quick housekeeping, and jumped in the shower. She acted like it was urgent that she saw me right away. I hoped it's the good kind of urgent, and not the bad. After filling the carousel k-cup assortment, I felt I was ready for her.

Five minutes later, my doorbell rang. I opened the door to find Tina with tears in her eyes. She looked terrible, like she hadn't slept a wink.

"Can I come in?"

"Of course! Tina, what's wrong.... why are you crying?" Tina began pacing nervously, back and forth in my living room. Apparently, she had been receiving some terrifying messages from her spirit guide. Messages that warned of impending doom. Our lives would be in danger if we continued to pursue the truth. I didn't know how to console her, so I just listened, and asked her to explain the danger that we were in.

"Jay, I don't know how much you know about the spirit world, but it's not like you see in the movies. It's all about love. Basically, if a medium is a good person, they will only attract good spirits. That has always held true to me until now. Does your family have any enemies that would want to hurt us?"

"No, none that I'm aware of. Well, wait a minute. That's not entirely true. In just this week, I've seen visions of two of my ancestors murdered by the same man. But that was many years ago. Certainly that man is no longer living."

"Does he have descendents?" asked Tina. She continued to pace the floor.

"I can't answer that. I don't even know his identity. Spirit gives me little snippets of information with every vision I have, but so far, the murderer remains anonymous."

"So, we just remain cautious and try to figure out who wants to hurt us, and why?" She was getting anxious and irritated, so much different from her usual bubbly self.

"I guess that's all we *can* do," I answered. Something else was wrong, though. I could sense it in the way she spoke, and even in the way she looked at me. She's probably trying to brush me off. This was more than she bargained for, and she's just trying to find a nice way to tell me to stay away from her. The suspense was killing me, so I had to make the first move. "Tina, is there something else bothering you? Something I did or said? Please be honest. If you don't want to be involved with this, I understand. You shouldn't have to feel scared because of my past."

Suddenly, Tina stopped pacing, pulled her hair back, away from her face, and looked into my eyes. "Jay, would you just shut up for a minute and let me speak?"

Oh boy, now I did it. "Sorry Tina, go ahead."

"I lied to you. I didn't have a date last night. The truth is, I think you're a great guy, and I wanted to spend more time with you, but I was scared."

"Scared of me?" I asked.

"No, not at all. Remember when I told you that I would know when the right guy comes along? Well, my spirit guide is telling me you might be that guy. I know it sounds weird because we just met, and we're both getting over bad relationships. It's crazy to rush things, and I haven't even asked about your feelings for me. It usually takes me a long time to open up and feel comfortable with someone. But you're different. I felt it the first time we met. I feel it every time we're together. I don't understand it, and it scares the hell out of me! Does any of this make sense to you?"

I couldn't believe what I was hearing! I had waited my whole life to meet a woman who had feelings and wasn't afraid or ashamed to share them. "Perfect sense! I feel it too. Just your smile, and listening to you speak is enough to brighten any room. The way you look at me and listen to me when I speak makes me feel important. I've never felt that way before. Please don't be afraid to share your feelings. I don't think I'd ever tire of hearing them. We don't have to rush into anything. We can take it slow and see what happens, okay?"

Tina smiled and walked close to me. As she reached out to give me a hug, she said, "Oh thank God....I've been a nervous wreck for the past two days. You've made me feel so much better!"

I've been hugged by other women, but never like this. I've never felt warmth, tenderness, and caring from a hug until now. It felt so good; I didn't want to let go. Finally, Tina stepped back, put a finger on my lips, and started listening.

"Jay, we need to go."

"Where?" I asked.

"Caleb is telling me that we have the correct map. We need to go to the address on that map and have a look around."

"Okay, let's go!"

This time, we took Petey.

Chapter 23

The address on the tax map was 277 Roberts Road. To get there, we had to drive west on Route 44 for about 4 miles, and make a right on to Roberts Road. My navigation app then said, 'After 3 miles, your destination is on the left.' I could remember, as a child, going fishing with my dad at a pond in that area. Who would have thought that my ancestors had lived near there?

When we arrived, the map on my phone said that we were actually closer to Aaron but still had a Ventura mailing address. I parked my car in a small pull-off on the right side of the road and got out.

"Are you sure we're at the right address?" asked Tina.

"Yeah, this is definitely it." Standing before us was a ten foot tall wooden fence, with an equally high steel chain-link fence outlining it. The outer fence had razor wire strung along the top, along with trees and vines tangled between the two fences. To our left was Roberts Creek, at which point, the fence made a ninety-degree turn to the right, and followed the creek as far as the eye could see. About twenty feet to our right was a gate, which was made of heavy steel and was kept closed with several chains and locks. The wooden interior fence had a gate which aligned with the outer gate and had an equally impressive lock system attached. There were tire tracks in the dirt leading up to the gates, which made it apparent that this entrance was used regularly. There was also an abundance of warning signs attached to the fences. 'No Trespassing' and 'Danger, Stay Out' were hanging every 20 feet or so. It would seem that the fences stretched to the right for at least a mile....maybe more.

Tina and I both stared at the fence and the surrounding area in disbelief. This was no longer a farm. Something had happened here, a long time ago.

"Jay, I'm speechless. I was expecting to see a farm, and maybe an old house, or a barn. Is this what Caleb wanted us to see? Or does he want us to discover what's on the other side of the fence?"

"I hope the spirit world can help us, because we can't go over the fence, and apparently we can't go around it. Whoever owns this property has something that no one else is supposed to see."

Tina took my hand in hers and tried to reassure me that everything would be okay. "Why don't you call Sue? Maybe she can find out who the current owner is."

"Good idea. I'll do that first thing Monday morning."

We got back in my car and proceeded down Roberts Road very slowly. While driving, I kept one eye on the fence, hoping to find a hole, or a weak spot, which would allow me access. The fence length along Roberts Road turned out to be 7/8 of a mile. At which point, it made a ninety-degree turn to the left. Again, it went as far as the eye could see. This was getting us nowhere, so I turned around and headed for home. Tina had dozed off. It was obvious that she was exhausted and needed some sleep.

While driving home, I kept thinking about the vision I had of Caleb in his fields shortly before his murder. The crops and the soil were perfect. There were no weeds, no vines, and no trees. What had happened? Maybe, if the fields were left unattended and not plowed or cultivated, over time it would become overgrown. That, I understand. But what the hell is that fence all about? I never saw a fence that tall, that went on and on and on.

When I pulled into my driveway, the first thing I saw was Kyle's pickup. There was no mistaking it. Covered in chrome, with oversized wheels and tires, and an exhaust so loud you need ear plugs to drive it. Kyle spent more on that truck than most people spend on a house.

As I was parking my car, Tina woke up. I placed my hand on

hers and said, "Kyle is here. Stay in the car, and I'll try to get rid of him, okay?"

Kyle was walking toward me with a huge smile etched on his face. I tried to get out and close the car door before he could see my passenger, but I wasn't fast enough.

"Hey buddy, I just stopped by to see how you're feeling!" He put his arm around me and led me away from my car. Pulling me close, and speaking in a very low tone, he said, "Is that the psychic lady in your car? She's got a killer body, but she's frigid. If you're trying to tap that, don't waste your time. I already tried."

"Kyle, for your information, Tina is a medium, and she's my friend. And no, I'm not trying to *tap* her. What's wrong...bored with Lisa already?"

"What are you talking about? There's nothing going on between me and Lisa."

"You're a terrible liar, and a terrible friend."

"Okay, if you're mad at me, I can understand that. But don't you think Lisa deserves a second chance? She loves you so much."

"No, I don't. I hope you two are happy and have a great life together. Now, leave me alone, and let me try to find some happiness."

Before leaving, Kyle asked when I would be returning to work. I replied, "Just as soon as hell starts freezing over." Without saying another word, he climbed into his truck and left. That was definitely an admission of guilt. If he was telling the truth, he would have argued, and maybe even hit me. I felt relieved to get that over with. The only bad part is, now I'm unemployed.

"Jay, I need to go home and get some sleep. Do you have any plans for this evening?"

"I was hoping to spend some time with you."

Tina seemed ecstatic. "Would you like to come to my place later? I can cook some dinner, and afterwards we could watch some movies. Sound good?"

"That sounds great! Shall I bring a bottle of wine?"

"Yes please. A Rose' would be nice. Say around 5:00?"

Tina texted me her address and drove away. Wow! This turned out to be a very eventful day.

Chapter 24

"Did you get enough to eat?" asked Tina.

"Oh my God, yes! It was great, but I can't eat another bite."

Tina had cooked a delicious dinner, comprising London Broil, baked potato, and string beans. Everything was perfect. The bottle of wine that I brought was actually Tina's favorite. After dinner, I helped clear the table and load the dishwasher, so we could retire to the living room.

Tina's apartment was beautiful and spacious. It has a large living room, with a sliding glass door leading to a balcony. There was an eat-in kitchen, dining room, two bedrooms, and a master bath with shower, tub, and double vanity. She must be making decent money as a medium to afford an apartment like this.

As Tina sat down next to me on the sofa, I couldn't help but stare at her. She was perfect. Outstanding personality, beautiful face and hair, and an awesome body. What more could a guy want?

"Why are you looking at me like that?"

"Like what?" I asked.

"I don't know. I guess I'm just self conscious about my appearance."

"Tina, you are beautiful! There's nothing to feel self conscious about."

"Thanks. You're not so bad yourself, you know." Tina smiled and kissed me gently on the lips.

Wow! It was just a quick, simple kiss, but it knocked my socks off. I had never felt so much passion in one small kiss.

"Who was the auto mechanic in your family?"

I came back down to earth and landed with a thud. "Excuse me?"

"Was someone in your family an auto mechanic? Your dad, maybe?"

"Yes. How did you know that?" My father was the owner of Thompson's Service on Main Street in Ventura. He could fix anything, and his customers loved him.

"He just told me."

Tears welled in my eyes as I thought about my dad. He worked his butt off, but always made time for his family. He loved to do things to make each of us feel special.

"So, you're kissing me and talking with my father at the same time?"

Tina laughed. "I didn't plan it that way. Sometimes messages come at awkward times."

I kissed Tina again. This one was deeper and lasted longer. "What else did he say?" I whispered.

Tina furrowed her brow and got serious. "He said to be very careful of Lisa and Kyle. They are very dangerous, and will stop at nothing to get what they want."

"And that is?"

Tina paused and closed her eyes. "It has something to do with money, but he's not exactly sure."

Their lives revolved around money, and I was so happy to get away from that madness. My stress levels were already coming down. I couldn't care less how large my bank account is, or how expensive my car is. I'm overjoyed if my bills are paid and there's a little left at the end of the month.

The next four hours were sheer delight. An action movie and a rom-com, holding Tina's hand all the while, and an occasional kiss, made it the best evening I ever had. All good things must come to an end though, so we said our goodbyes around midnight, and I headed for home.

My only thoughts all the way home were of Tina. Because

of her, I almost didn't care about finding my family's secrets. Maybe I should just forget about my family tree. Perhaps all of my family members died of accidents, or natural causes. Letting go of the past and concentrating on the present just might be the right thing to do.

Arriving home, I parked my car and walked to my apartment door. A voice behind me called my name. When I turned to see who it was, someone with a fist the size of a cantaloupe hit me right between the eyes. I blacked out for a few seconds and fell to my knees. There were two guys, both wearing ski masks. The first one had hit me, and the second one kicked me in the ribs, not once, but twice. I fell forward, writhing in pain, not knowing who was kicking my ass or why.

Finally, the first one spoke. "Stay away from Roberts Road, Jason. Next time, we won't be so gentle." They took off on foot, and ran half a block before they got in their car, and drove away.

That voice....I knew that voice. Just couldn't place it right now. I limped to my apartment, got undressed, and cleaned up. There was no point in calling the cops. They wouldn't be able to help me. All I wanted right now was sleep.

Chapter 25

Sunday was a painful day. I spent most of the day in bed, with ice packs on my ribs and face, and lots of ibuprofen. My left eye was black, and my nose was swollen to three times its normal size. Everything from the night before was still very foggy, but the voice I heard was very familiar to me.

It was around 3:00pm when my phone rang. It was Tina.

"Hi Jay. Sorry to bother you. Just calling to see how your day is going?"

I let out a moan as I tried to sit up. "It's ok I guess. How are you?"

"Oh my God, you sound terrible! What's wrong?"

"I had a welcoming committee waiting for me last night. They rearranged my nostrils, and my ribcage."

"Wait, what? You're not making any sense. What are you talking about?"

"Two guys beat me up when I got home. Told me to stay away from Roberts Road."

"Oh, no! That's terrible. Stay put. I'll be there shortly and drive you to the ER."

"Wait Tina, no ....I don't want..." But she had already hung up.

Suddenly, a terrible thought entered my brain. While we were on Roberts road, I can't remember seeing any cars drive by us. So, how did the two bullies know I had been there? Who else knew of my whereabouts on Saturday? Tina did.

No, that's impossible. Tina is for real. She cares about me and wouldn't do anything to hurt me. There has to be an explanation, but whoever did this to me obviously knows me, and knows where I live. Maybe they have security cameras installed on the fence posts. Yes, that would explain it.

A few minutes later, my doorbell rang. Now I had the unenviable task of convincing Tina that I was fine and didn't require a trip to the hospital. I opened my apartment door only to come face to face with Lisa. She looked just as bad as I did. Maybe worse....she had a black eye and a fat lip. When our eyes met, we both burst out laughing, and almost simultaneously said, "What the hell happened to you?" It was the first laughter that she and I had shared in a long time. I wasn't mad at Lisa. It just felt good to accept the fact that I was no longer in love with her.

We both shared stories of our injuries, but it was obvious that neither of us was telling the truth. Lisa also explained that she had stopped by to pick up some of her things.

"Lisa, this isn't easy to say, but I have been seeing someone. She's on her way here now, so maybe it would be easier on all of us if you weren't here when she arrives."

"Not wasting any time, are you? That's ok, I can't blame you. I'm no better than you. I'll call you tomorrow and arrange a time to come get my things."

I thanked Lisa and gave her a hug. I almost felt sorry for her. Something had happened. This wasn't the same Lisa that I've known for so long. Something, or someone, had hurt her, and taken some of the life out of her. I just hope that Kyle hadn't hurt her.

Several moments later, my doorbell rang again. This time, it was Tina. I could see the shock on her face when she looked at me. "Oh my God, Jay! What did they do to you?" She hugged me and squeezed tight. I flinched in pain and pushed her away. Realizing what she had done, she apologized and offered to drive me to the ER.

"No thanks, I'll be ok. Just need some rest. And maybe some dinner?"

Tina laughed, "You got it. What are you in the mood for?"

That was an open-ended question, and I would have answered her in some perverted way if I wasn't in so much pain. So, instead, I opted for burgers and fries. Besides, that was all I had in the freezer.

After dinner, I got comfortable on the couch, and turned on the TV. Tina made sure I had everything I needed, and left for home at 9:00. She wanted to stay, but had to keep an appointment with a client early on Monday morning.

Honestly, I was a little disappointed with the amount of help that Tina had provided. I was expecting a lot of communication with spirit, and messages from Caleb, Will, and my dad. But, so far, not much. Maybe I just need to be more patient.

I could feel the ibuprofen kicking in as I became drowsy. Drifting off to sleep, I started *hearing* telepathic messages from my spirit guide. "Jason, don't trust anyone." It played in my head over and over. Opening my eyes, the same blurry outline of a hooded man slowly faded into the darkness. I can't deal with this much longer. My life is turning into a real shit show. Tina is the only good thing in my life right now. Why me?? I mind my own business. I don't hurt anyone. Live and let live is my motto. Why can't people (and spirits) just leave me alone?

Chapter 26

In July 1950, Thomas Bowen's wife, Estelle, passed away from breast cancer. There were many people in Ventura that said losing his wife pushed Thomas over the edge. He became even more egotistical and self-centered than ever before. Hazel, 16, and Thomas Jr, 12, were his children, but he had no feelings for them. It was easier to pay other people to raise his kids than to do it himself. Hazel and TJ despised their father and seldom spoke with him.

Hazel had a difficult time dealing with the loss of her mother. They had been very close. As Thomas ran the farm on a daily basis, Hazel and Estelle would play games, go for drives in the country, and take long walks through the fields. Estelle made Hazel feel safe and loved. After Estelle had passed, Hazel tried to fill that void in her life. She began dating, but Thomas would scare off any boy that got close with Hazel. Threatening to kill any boy that hurt his daughter was an effective means of keeping unwanted young men away from his family.

Hazel graduated from Ventura High in 1952. She had never shown any interest in college, but when Thomas offered to pay her tuition, she jumped at the opportunity to get away from her father, and enrolled at The University of Illinois. Hazel was definitely not the scholarly type, but she wasn't there for an education. The attention and affection she received from the young men she dated satisfied her desires for love. Even if it was only short-lived. She knew how to attract the attention of any guy she wanted and enjoyed doing so. Blond hair, blue eyes, the perfect hourglass figure, and long, smooth legs. She had it all. The only thing she lacked was enough common sense to use birth control. She became pregnant in November 1952. Hazel had had multiple partners, so she didn't know who the father was. The pregnancy wasn't a problem at first. Loose clothing can hide a lot. And if anyone asked, she joked she needed to quit eating so much junk food. To hide the pregnancy from her father, she told him she would be taking summer classes and needed some extra cash for her tuition and housing. Thomas thought this was a promising sign. Maybe his little girl was finally maturing and taking her education seriously.

The only thing that Hazel was taking seriously was her pregnancy. She could feel a life inside of her, and she loved that feeling. It made her think of her mother and the bond that they shared. She wanted to create that same type of bond with her child. Unfortunately, she never had the chance. In July of that year, Thomas paid an unexpected visit to Hazel's dorm room. By this time, she was 8 months pregnant and could no longer hide her condition. Hazel could see the anger on Thomas's face when he gazed upon her body.

"Daddy, I can explain." The fear of her father was clear as her voice quivered.

"Can you? Well, you'll have plenty of time for explanations on the way home."

"No Daddy, I don't want to go. I'd rather stay...."

Without warning, Thomas punched Hazel with a roundhouse right to the face, which knocked her to the floor. Before she could react, Thomas kicked her in the mid-section with all his might. The pain was so intense, she couldn't even scream. Grabbing a handful of hair, he dragged her out to his car, threw her in the back seat, and drove away, leaving all of her possessions behind. Hazel passed out shortly after their departure. The pain was too great to bear.

Upon their return to Ventura, TJ ran to the car to greet them. "Oh my God, Dad, what happened? Hazel's bleeding badly!" There was indeed a large puddle of blood on the back seat of Thomas's Cadillac.

"Your sister has had an accident. Help her to her room, and I'll call Doc Blanchard."

Dr. Henry Blanchard, along with his wife Jane, arrived at the Bowen house 20 minutes later. TJ led them up to Hazel's room, where they spent the next several hours. Jane made several trips downstairs to collect towels, a bucket of hot water, and a large canvas sack. While all of this was going on, Thomas sat in his rocking chair on the front porch, smoking a cigar and reading the newspaper. Finally, Doc Blanchard joined him on the porch.

"She'll be ok, Tom, after a few weeks of bed rest. I'm sorry, but we couldn't save the baby. Eh, what happened to her, anyway?"

"Accident. What did you do with it?"

"TJ put the body in a canvas sack. I think he took it out to the barn."

"Thanks for coming, Doc. I'll appreciate your discretion in this matter."

Doc Blanchard was appalled at the cold-blooded behavior of Thomas, but was afraid of the consequences he would face if he revealed anything to the authorities. "Certainly, Tom."

"Send me your bill, Doc. And if you see TJ on your way out, tell him to burn it."

Chapter 27

I arrived at the Crandall County Courthouse at 8:00am Monday morning. Carrying two coffees into Sue's office, I was hoping to bribe her again. Things were bustling at such an early hour, but this time, no bribes were necessary. When I limped through her doorway, and Sue saw the condition I was in, she stopped what she was doing and ran to my side. I knew she would help me in any way that she could, but it wouldn't come without a little ball-busting.

"Did Tina beat you up already? Wow, it didn't take her long to get to know you!"

I tried to smile, but it hurt my nose too much. "I can always count on you for words of encouragement." Sue gave me a hug, but I winced at the pain it caused.

"Ooh, I'm sorry Jay. What happened? You look terrible!"

I told her the complete story of my visit to Roberts Road, and the consequences that I suffered later that day. Sue was unaware of the fence surrounding the property at 277 Roberts Road, and couldn't think of a reason anyone would want to be so secretive.

"So, how did these thugs know you were on Roberts Road?"

"I have no idea," I replied.

"While you were pulled over, they must have driven past."

"Maybe, but I don't remember seeing any other cars going by while we were there."

Sue stared at me with a pessimistic look on her face. "Are you sure you can trust Tina?"

"Sure, I'm sure. Well, pretty sure anyway. What are you thinking, Sue?"

"Nothing. Just be careful. You've only known her for a short time."

I hung my head low. I really didn't want to get into this discussion today.

Sue changed the subject. "Anyway, I know this isn't a social call, so how can I help you today?"

"I need to know who the current owner of that property is. Maybe they can tell me what I need to know."

"And exactly what is it you need to know?"

"You wouldn't believe me if I told you."

"You're probably right. I'll look up the owner of that property, but I want you to talk with Sheriff Booker and tell him exactly what happened to you Saturday evening. His office is down at the end of the hall, on the left. I'll call and tell him you're on your way."

"Okay. Thanks Sue."

I made my way down to Sheriff Booker's office and had a long chat with him. I filled out a half dozen reports and told him everything that happened over the weekend. Minus the communication with spirit....I don't think he'd understand. Honestly, I don't understand all of it. The Sheriff said he would have one of his deputies do some digging and see what he could come up with. I thanked him and returned to Sue's office.

"There he is, the great comedian!" Sue welcomed me back to her office. At least I think it was a welcome.

"What are you talking about?" Her remark completely dumbfounded me.

"I'm talking about you, sending me off on a wild goose chase. Do you think I have nothing better to do?"

"Sue, what the hell are you talking about? I would never do anything to waste your time."

"Okay, I'll take your word for it. So, hold on to your socks. The owner of that property is....you. The title was transferred to you when your father passed away."

My jaw hit the floor when Sue shared the news with me. Needless to say, this was not what I was expecting at all.

"I don't get it. My father owned a house and an auto repair shop in Ventura. He would have told me if he owned any other property. That's crazy! How could I own any property? I've never set foot on it, and I've paid no taxes on it!"

"Well, the taxes have been paid in full for the past twenty years. The records show you are the sole owner of that property. In fact, ownership has never left the Thompson family. Caleb left it to Will, Will to Charles, and Charles to you."

I didn't know what else to say. None of this made any sense to me. If the property never left the Thompson family ownership, why did we stop farming? And who built the massive fence encircling the fields? I wonder if Caleb and Flora's house is still standing? I can't tell with the fence and the overgrown trees and shrubs blocking the view. Just then, Sheriff Booker stepped into Sue's office.

"Sheriff, can we have a few moments with you?" asked Sue.

Sue explained the discovery she just made, and Sheriff Booker gazed at her with disbelief in his eyes.

"Sue, I don't mean to be rude, but what you're saying makes absolutely no sense, right?" replied Sheriff Booker. "How can a citizen own property, and pay taxes on said property, but be totally unaware of it?"

Sue didn't have a logical explanation to share with the Sheriff. "I know it sounds crazy, but I don't have any other explanation."

"Does this mean I can tear down that ridiculous fence and see what's being hidden?" I asked.

"Whoa Jason, not so fast. You'll have to do a title search first, to make sure there are no liens or back taxes due on the property."

"Okay, how do I do that?" I asked.

"Find yourself a good real estate attorney," said Sue. "They'll take care of everything for you."

I thanked Sue and Sheriff Booker for their help and headed for home. I needed more ibuprofen.

Chapter 28

Hazel spent the next few weeks in her bedroom. The pain in her abdomen went away slowly, but the mental anguish that she felt would never go away. The feeling of a new life inside of her had made her feel full of life. In a way, it felt as if her mother's spirit was to be reborn in her baby's body. As odd as that sounds, it made perfect sense to Hazel. However, her father had put an end to her dreams.

Thomas Bowen desired three things in life: power, wealth, and control. These traits were worthless if he couldn't show them for everyone to see. By taking the life of his daughter's unborn baby, he had again proved how much power he held in his community and the amount of control he had over his family. His daughter, however, possessed the same desires he held so near and dear, with one additional trait...revenge.

It was early autumn when Hazel felt well enough to get some exercise. She started slowly, taking short walks around the neighborhood. The exercise and fresh air helped to clear her mind, giving her a chance to think and decide what she should do next with her life. Gradually, she increased the distance she walked. Little by little she reached new plateaus....one mile, two miles, three miles. One sunny Saturday morning, she decided to try a five-mile walk. At the three-mile mark, she came upon the home of Will and Mary Thompson. Mary, being 7 months pregnant, was lounging in a lawn chair, under a tree in her front yard. As Hazel got close, she stopped to say hello.

Mary smiled and said, "Good morning. You're Hazel Bowen, right? I'm Mary Thompson."

That's all it took. Hazel gave up on the rest of her walk that day. She sat with Mary and discussed anything and everything associated with pregnancies and babies. They hit it off right from the start. Hazel told Mary she lost her baby, but was planning on trying again very soon. Mary didn't inquire about the baby's father. She didn't feel it was any of her business. The two women spent the rest of the afternoon chatting, laughing, and sipping iced tea. It was a day that they both enjoyed and decided to do it again the following Saturday. Hazel left there late in the afternoon, overjoyed that she had finally met a decent person with a personality much like her mother's. Mary was also happy to have someone to talk to. She and Will hadn't been communicating very well since the death of his father Caleb several months ago.

When Hazel returned home, Thomas was sitting in his rocker on the front porch of his home. The malicious look on his face was enough to warn Hazel that she was in trouble. But, then again, she was always in trouble with her father.

"Where have you been?" Thomas demanded an answer.

"I don't think it's any of your business," she replied.

"Look, if you're living under my roof, then it is my business. I brought you home from college because you were living off of my money, and spreading your legs for any guy that showed you a little attention. You haven't been contributing to any of the household chores, so if you're not happy here, you can pack your bags and get out! But you'll never get another dime from me."

"I don't want your money. Don't you understand anything about life? I had a mother who loved me with all of her heart. Her love was unconditional. It was a good, pure love. The love a parent should have for their child. I did my best to return that love to her. I wanted her to know how special she was, and how special she made me feel. We had that bond. I guess it's too much to ask for the same with you." Hazel laid all of her cards on the table, but to no avail. Her father simply was not capable of loving anyone but himself.

In a cold, heartless reply, Thomas said, "One week. I'll give you one week to get your things together and get out. TJ can help you pack."

She turned away from him and said sternly, "No need. I'll be out tomorrow."

Chapter 29

"**I**s that what you think, Jay? Do you really think I would do anything to hurt you? I thought we were building something special, but maybe I'm wrong?"

"No, Tina, wait a minute. I only asked if you had told anyone about our outing on Saturday. I'm not accusing you of anything, just trying to cover all my bases. Please don't be mad at me." Maybe it's me. Maybe I don't know how to communicate effectively. It seems like I'm always putting my foot in my mouth.

"I'm not mad. I just misunderstood what you were asking me. Let's forget it, ok? No worries, all is good!"

I extended my arms to give Tina a hug, but she pulled me close and planted a deep, wet kiss on my lips. She was wearing a thin silk blouse and a pair of black leggings. I could tell she wasn't wearing a bra or panties. As she pushed her body against mine, I began backpedaling, losing my balance, and landing on my sofa. Tina followed and landed on top of me, straddling and grinding against me. Having her body against mine felt amazing, and I wanted so badly for it to go further. However, my conscience stepped in and said 'no'.

"Tina," I whispered in her ear.

She stopped kissing my neck long enough to say, "Shhhh."

"Tina, I can't."

"Sure, you can," she said as she began unbuttoning my shirt.

"No, I can't. I'm not ready for this yet. It's too early. I want this relationship to last, and I think we should build it slowly." I pushed her away from me, expecting her to be angry. Instead, she smiled with a warm glow in her eyes.

"You're right, Jay. You're absolutely right. I'm sorry, I should have known better." Tina got off of me and sat next to me on the sofa, holding my hand. "I think you're the first guy I ever met who had the willpower to say 'no'."

Those words made me feel proud, but it also made me wonder how many other guys she's been with that hadn't said no. What started as a friendly visit quickly turned into much more. As I looked at Tina, all I could think of was Sue asking me if I could trust her. Maybe it's just my anxiety, but I'm having a hard time trusting anyone.

We went to the kitchen table, where I poured two cups of coffee, and I brought out my photo album. After showing Tina all the photos of my family, I asked if she had received any messages from spirit.

"Unfortunately, no I haven't. Don't be discouraged, though. Things have been crazy for the past week. Maybe we just need to get back to basics, meet at my office, and spend some quiet time with spirit. I'm free tomorrow afternoon, if you'd like to meet me there."

"Sure, I don't have any plans. I can bring the photo album. Maybe that will help." Tina flipped through the pages of photos, but my eyes were drawn to her low-cut blouse and incredibly sexy cleavage. Damn it, why do I have to have a conscience?

*   *   *

"Sheriff, is it really necessary to bother me while I'm working?" James Bowen had little regard for the law in Crandall County, feeling that he was above it.

Sheriff Booker despised James, and the whole Bowen family, for that matter. "I'm sorry to disturb you, James, but there's something I need to share with you. It seems that Jason Thompson has learned of his ownership of the property on Roberts Road."

"Well, how the hell did that happen, Sheriff? Did you tell

him?"

"I haven't told him anything. In fact, I just met him. He came into my office to report a couple of thugs had beat him up and warned him about returning to Roberts Road. You wouldn't know anything about that, would you?"

"No, that's news to me." He refused to make eye contact with Sheriff Booker.

"Just remember, James, this is above you and me. Crandall County and the State of Illinois have records of ownership. I can't do anything to change that. And if anything should happen to Jason Thompson, you'll be the first person I pay a visit to. Do you understand?"

"Don't you dare threaten me, Sheriff! You're in this just as deep as I am. I bet the Illinois State Police would love to hear where you got the money for your in-ground swimming pool and your new SUV."

"You've got an enormous set of balls, James. The inmates at the state penitentiary would love to get you alone," said Sheriff Booker as he stormed out of the village hall and slammed the door behind him.

James got up from his desk and began to pace the floor of his office. He knew this day would be coming. It was inevitable. He just had to put his faith in Lisa and hope that she could patch things up with Jason.

Chapter 30

Hazel squeezed all of her basic necessities into the largest suitcase she could find and put all her weight on it so TJ could close the latches. She knew things were going to be difficult for a while, but the peace of mind she needed would come much easier once away from her father.

"Where will you go?" asked TJ.

"I'm not sure. Maybe back to college. I have friends there who might let me stay with them for a while. And I could apply for a scholarship. TJ, I'm not worried about the future. I'll be okay, and believe me when I say that someday I will get revenge on him, for what he did to me....for what he did to my baby."

"When that day comes, I'll be there for you."

Hazel brushed a tear from her cheek, grabbed her purse and suitcase, and walked out to TJ's pickup truck. Thomas had given TJ permission to drive Hazel to the bus stop in Ventura, but not one inch further. She expected nothing less from her father.

Will and Mary Thompson's house was on the way to the bus stop, and as they approached it, Hazel could see Mary watering the flowers that outlined her front porch.

"Pull over here, TJ. I want to say goodbye to a friend."

"But I have to get back soon, or Dad will have my ass."

"It's okay, you can go. I'll walk the rest of the way." Hazel leaned over, gave TJ a hug, and promised to keep in touch.

Hazel exited the truck, and Mary was surprised to see her toting such a large suitcase. It was immediately obvious that something was very wrong.

"Well, hello there Hazel. Are you going on a vacation?"

A chuckle was mixed with a few tears as Hazel approached

Mary.

"I stopped by to say goodbye, Mary. I enjoyed spending time with you yesterday, and I didn't want to leave without thanking you and Will for your hospitality."

"That's so sweet, Hazel. But where are you going?"

Not wanting to be a burden to anyone, Hazel tried to convince Mary that she was returning to college. It was painfully obvious that Hazel was not being truthful about her intentions, for she was having trouble holding back the tears. Will joined the ladies in the front yard and listened to the end of Hazel's story.

Mary felt it was her duty to ask, "Are you sure this is what you want? And be truthful, honey."

"Right now, I'm not sure about anything." She finally quit trying to suppress the tears, and began sobbing uncontrollably.

Mary gave Will an inquisitive stare, and he knew exactly what she was thinking. He nodded his head as if to say it was okay, and he turned and walked away.

"Hazel, you know the baby will be coming soon, and I'm going to need some help around here. Will is always so busy on the farm, and I can't take care of everything else by myself. Why don't you stay here with us for a while? We can't afford to pay you much, but you'd have free room and board, and free meals. And there's three spare bedrooms upstairs. You pick the one you like the most. So, what do you say?"

"Oh my God! I would love to live here with you, and help with the baby! It would make me so happy! But, I'm afraid of what my father might do. I don't want him causing any trouble for you guys."

"Look, Caleb and Flora weren't afraid of your father. And Will and I have no fear of him, either. So stop worrying and tell me you'll stay."

Hazel wiped the tears from her eyes, wrapped her arms around Mary, and squeezed her tightly. With a big, beautiful smile, she graciously declared, "Yes! Yes, I'll stay! Thank you so, so much!"

Chapter 31

"So, Mr. Thompson, I'm going to email some forms to you. They're in pdf format, so just fill them out and send them back to us, with payment, and we'll get the ball rolling. It shouldn't take too long to get you an answer."

Patty, the legal assistant at Gibson Law Firm, was very helpful. I'm glad I phoned. "Sounds good….if you need any other information, Sue at the County Clerk's office might be able to help you."

"Will do. Talk with you soon, Mr. Thompson!"

God, I hate when people call me Mr. Thompson. It makes me feel so old. I don't act old. Maybe I look old. But Patty doesn't know what I look like. We just spoke on the phone. Holy shit, what the hell is wrong with me??! Anxiety sucks, big time. There are times I wish I could hop in my car, drive away, and never look back. Who knows? Maybe I'll do that when this is over with. In the meantime, though, I'm stuck here.

A knock on my apartment door was Lisa. "Hey, come on in. Want some coffee?"

"Sure. Am I disturbing you? I could come back at another time."

I cleared some papers off the kitchen table and pulled out a chair. "No, not at all. Have a seat."

Lisa and I sat and talked and had a really pleasant visit. We even joked about the bruises on our faces healing, but neither one of us would admit how we received these injuries. I even got up the nerve to ask if Kyle had hit her, but she said no.

"Jason, I screwed up and cheated on you. I admit that.

Probably because I felt that our relationship was going nowhere. I was stupid, and should have been more patient. I'm sorry for what I've done. Kyle and I broke up yesterday. He and I were not right for each other."

"I'm sorry to hear that." I wasn't sorry one bit, but it felt so good to listen to her grovel and admit she made a mistake.

"As hard as it must be to believe this, I still love you and would do anything for a second chance with you."

"I think you and I both know that would never work."

I gave Lisa all of her things she had left in my apartment and told her I would see her around town.

"That's not likely. I'm unemployed....got fired this morning. So, I'm thinking of moving to Chicago. That's as good a place as any to make a fresh start. Be careful Jason. And call if you ever need me."

Wow, her own father fired Lisa. It doesn't get any worse than that.

*   *   *

I arrived at Tina's office at 1:00pm and knocked on her door.

"Come on in, silly! You don't need to knock," Tina shouted from the other side of the door.

I walked in to find Tina seated on the couch, wearing a short black skirt, stockings, and a lacey, red see-thru shirt with a black bra underneath. I couldn't help but stare.

"What? Is there something wrong?"

"I swear you're trying to seduce me. You look sexier every time I see you!"

"I'm sorry, I could change if you don't like it?"

"No, you're fine. Believe me, you are very fine!"

I sat on the couch next to her and gave her a quick kiss on the lips. Tina didn't let go, though, and gave me a much longer kiss than I was expecting.

"So, should we get started?" Tina whispered seductively in my ear.

She took my hand in hers and bowed her head to say an opening prayer. Asking God to help us and allow Spirit to communicate with us made me feel good. Having God on our side had to be a good thing, right? After the prayer, Tina sat quietly for a few moments. Finally, she looked me in the eye and told me that Caleb was speaking to her. Caleb's message was frightening, saying that it was Lisa's family that had been murdering members of my family for many years. And Lisa and Kyle were planning on doing away with us soon. This seemed odd to me. I know little about the events of the past, but as for now, Kyle backed off when we had words, and Lisa seems to have realized her mistakes. When I asked why they would want to hurt us, she began crying, and shouted, "I don't know! Caleb doesn't know! It's all so frightening. Hold me Jay, please hold me!"

I wrapped my arms around her and held her tight. "Shhh… everything is ok. I won't let anyone hurt you." A few seconds later, her eyes met mine.

"Oh, Jay…" Our lips joined, and she thrust her tongue deep into my mouth. "I want you so badly, baby," she whispered in my ear.

This wasn't fair. I couldn't keep fighting these desires. I think I wanted her even more than she wanted me. But how could someone go from being so frightened to being so horny, in the blink of an eye?

Tina lay back on the couch and pulled me on top of her. Feeling her body under mine felt incredible, but it was nothing compared to the moment she reached down and pulled up her skirt, so that she could wrap her legs around me. She was wearing stockings and garters, but no panties. Feeling the heels of her pumps digging into my calves, I knew I couldn't control myself much longer. I never thought I would be with a woman who turned me on more than Lisa, but now I knew differently.

Suddenly, everything came to a screeching halt. The voice of my Spirit Guide spoke to me in a clear, concise voice. There was no mistaking this message.

"Seek the truth, Jason. Go home and prepare yourself."

What did that mean? I thought Tina was telling me the truth, but now I was feeling a chill rush over me. I didn't know exactly what was happening, or how I was feeling, but I could sense evil in the air.

I rolled off her and jumped to my feet. "I have to go."

"Wait Jay, where are you going? Did I say something wrong?"

I had to get out of there. I could feel my heart racing and my blood pressure rising. Before leaving, I looked back at the sexiest woman I've ever met, lying on her back, with her skirt pulled up to her waist. Even with all of those turn-ons, I knew I must run from her. I needed to go home and prepare for the truth.

Chapter 32

Mary had a difficult pregnancy. Constant morning sickness led to dehydration and several other health problems for herself and her unborn child. At 24 weeks, she developed gestational diabetes, which put even more stress on her body. Constant exhaustion and mood swings put a strain on her relationship with Will. At times, they would go days without speaking to one another.

Hazel could see what all of this was doing to Mary, so she tried to help in every way possible. Cooking, cleaning, shopping, and taking Mary to her doctor appointments were just a few of the many chores she handled daily. Knowing how busy Will was , she also tried to help him in any way possible. Running errands, picking up supplies, seed, and fertilizer kept her extremely busy.

March 14, 1954 was the big day as Mary gave birth to a healthy baby boy and named him Gregory Thompson. Once again, Hazel was there for Mary every step of the way. Driving her to the hospital, holding her hand, coaching her on, and reminding her to breathe. These were things that Will should have been doing. However, he showed little interest in Mary, or the baby. Apparently, he had other things on his mind. Things he didn't discuss with Mary. In fact, after Greg was born, the only communication between Will and Mary was in the form of arguments. Sadly, every argument between the two of them ended with Mary crying and yelling how sorry she was.

When Greg was two months old, Will and Mary stopped speaking to each other altogether. Hazel continued to do everything she could to make the Thompson family happy, but nothing seemed to help. So, instead, she concentrated on caring for the baby. She loved little Greg and protected him from the stress at home. Every day, she did her chores and cared for the baby, but did her best to stay away from both Will and Mary. The stress in the Thompson house was overwhelming. For the life of her, Hazel could not understand how such a beautiful marriage could fall apart so quickly.

On June 20th of that year, Mary went for a walk. It was 11:00am and she couldn't have picked a more gorgeous day, with lots of sunshine and a refreshing, cool breeze. Before leaving, she informed Hazel that she'd be back in about an hour.

In the meantime Hazel opened the windows, and let the house air out. After playing with Greg for a few minutes, she fixed his bottle and laid him down for a nap. Meal planning and cooking were two more chores that Hazel had taken on. Even though the dining room table never had the family seated for dinner, she wanted to make sure everyone had decent meals. That evening, it would be stuffed pork chops and fresh asparagus. By the time she finished the meal prep and got Greg up from his nap, it was nearly 2:00pm. It was then that she realized Mary had not yet returned from her walk. Seeing how beautiful a day it was, Hazel didn't worry. Mary must have been enjoying her walk and lost track of time.

Will arrived home at 6:00pm to the sweet aroma of pork chops cooking in the oven. But a concerned look on Hazel's face greeted him.

"What's wrong?" asked Will.

"Mary went for a walk this morning, and hasn't returned yet. I'm worried, Will. Where could she be?"

"Did she say where she was going?"

"No, only that she was going for a walk and would be back in about an hour." Hazel was panicking.

"Okay, take it easy. You call the police, and I'll go for a drive to find her. She couldn't have gone too far."

Hazel ran to the phone and dialed the Ventura Police Dept. She was politely informed that it was a Crandall County matter. So, she dialed the Crandall County Sheriff's office, and was told that it was too soon to start a missing person investigation. They had to wait a full twenty-four hours before that could be started.

Will returned home at 8:00pm with the smell of alcohol on his breath. Looking thoughtless, and possibly a bit drunk, he said that he covered the entire county, but his search turned up nothing. Without asking Hazel how she made out contacting the police, Will simply said that he was going to bed, and would look again in the morning. Hazel was flabbergasted! She understood that Will and Mary had been having marital problems, but his wife was missing! The mother of his son was missing, and he couldn't care less!

Chapter 33

Driving home, I continued to replay in my mind everything that had happened in Tina's office. She is, without a doubt, the sexiest, most desirable woman I've ever met. When I'm with her, I'm powerless to resist her. It's not just the physical aspect, either. She has a magnetic personality, which gives me the desire to be with her constantly. Yet, when my Spirit Guide spoke to me, it was a message powerful enough to completely change my thoughts. The message was simple and basic, however; it commanded me to do what I was told, for I knew I was listening to the truth. So, if Spirit was conveying the truth, what has Tina been sharing with me? At first, I thought I could trust her. Now, I'm seeing her in a different light.

After arriving home, I poured myself a glass of wine and got comfortable in my recliner. Leaving the blinds closed, I tried to relax. Was it wrong to feel betrayed? Why does it feel like I can no longer trust anyone? I'm feeling that both Lisa and Tina want something from me. But what could it be? Money? I laughed out loud. Hardly! I'm broke and need to look for a job soon. If things don't change quickly, I could be homeless as well.

A second glass of wine helped me to relax, but it was the third glass that made it possible to close my eyes and drift off to sleep....

"Mary, I warned you! I told you to stay out of it and mind your own business. You wouldn't listen, though. You were stubborn. So, now it's time to wipe those tears and move on." The same maniacal

killer that had ended the life of Caleb, now had his hands wrapped tightly around this woman's neck. As he squeezed the life out of her, she screamed and cried and begged for mercy, but to no avail.

Suddenly, a voice said, "Jason, do you know who those people are?"

The voice of Spirit called to me, but there was no one there. "The man is the same person who murdered my great-grandfather Caleb, but I can never see his face."

"You have seen visions of the woman before. She is the woman who is always...."

"Crying! I knew she looked familiar. Can't we help her?"

"No. This is a vision of an event that occurred long ago."

Finally, I asked the identity of this woman.

"This was your grandmother, Mary Kallas Thompson. Now you know why she's always crying."

"I never met her. She was Grandpa Will's wife. I was told that she must have run off with another man."

"That was not the case. She was murdered and her body was disposed of. There was no trace of her anywhere." Spirit reported the grim details of her death.

A bell began ringing in the distance. It was barely audible at first, but gradually became louder and closer. Over and over it rang. Louder and louder, until finally I realized it was....

My doorbell! Whoever was ringing my doorbell certainly was persistent. I pulled myself up out of the recliner, but nearly fell on my ass when I tried to stand. Three glasses of wine in a man that normally doesn't drink more than one glass in a week can make that man very drunk, very quickly. Meanwhile, my doorbell continued to chime.

"I'm coming! Hold your horses, damn it!" I stubbed my toe on the coffee table and nearly fell again. By this time, it was getting dark, and I couldn't find the wall switch for my living room lights. Finally, I made it to my front door, and turned on the living room and front porch lights. As I opened the door, I thought I was still dreaming. Standing on my front stoop was a middle-aged woman covered in freckles, with the brightest red hair I'd ever seen. I had to look down to get a good look at her. She was about 4 foot 6 inches tall, and if I had to guess, somewhere in the area of 250 pounds. She was wearing a yellow and white striped maxi-dress, and a pair of yellow crocs.

"Can I help you?" I was hoping she had the wrong address.

"Good evening, sir. I'm looking for Jason Thompson. Would that be you?" She was polite *and* well-spoken.

"That depends....who wants to know?"

"I do. So are you Mr. Thompson?"

There's that damn 'Mister' again. "Who are you?"

"I'm Amber Crystal."

"Your name is Amber Crystal?"

"Yes, sir. I'm a medium."

"Oh God, not another one." I tried to get rid of her, because I had to pee really bad. "Look, I'm not interested in whatever it is you're selling."

She insisted she wasn't selling anything, but had three messages for me.

"Would you like to hear them?"

"Messages from who?"

"Three spirits. I only know their first names. So, would you like to hear them?"

I shrugged. "Sure, why not? Come on in."

Amber entered my apartment, and after doing a quick look around, walked directly to the kitchen, where she seated herself at the kitchen table. I followed her and joined her at the table. Her hair seemed to reflect the light and gave my entire kitchen a reddish glow.

She began speaking, "First of all, let me start by saying this has never happened to me before. My spirit guide brought these three spirits to me and asked me to help them communicate with you. Apparently, something or someone has been blocking their messages. They only provided me with their first names. I know nothing else about who they are or how they relate to you. So, let's begin, shall we? The first spirit's name is Caleb. He wanted me to say he's sorry for scaring you and causing you to fall down. He was afraid you would be mad at him, so he left and asked another spirit to take his place. Do you understand this?"

I knew she was speaking of the first time Caleb was in my office. "Yes. How do you know about this?"

"He told me. Second spirit's name is Mary. She apologized for leaving you in the diner. It made you look crazy, speaking with dead people. Do you understand this?"

This time I recalled seeing my grandmother at the Ventura Diner. "Yes. But how do you know about this?"

"She told me. She also said you forgot to leave a tip for Gloria. You should go back and do that."

This is getting weird. "I'll put it on my list of things to do."

"The third spirit's name is Greg. Greg said the night of the fire, he chased a stranger from his home. When he got outside, he realized the house was fully engulfed in flames, so he went back in to rescue his family. He feels the stranger must have set the fire. Do you understand this?"

This was the most difficult message to receive. I didn't know that my dad had made it out of the house, but went back in to save his loved ones. And, until now, I didn't know that someone had set the fire. I began crying , and couldn't stop. In the past hour, I had witnessed the murders of my grandmother, parents, and brother. Who would want to do all this killing? And why my family? We're not rich. We have nothing of any value. Maybe this is why Spirit told me to go home. This strange little lady was obviously the real deal. There is no way she could have known all these things if she wasn't.

"Thank you for sharing this with me."

"It's my pleasure, sir." She handed me a business card with her name and phone number, and told me to call if she could do anything else to help me.

I walked her to the door, bent over to give her a hug, and told her I would definitely be calling. As she was driving away, Tina pulled into my driveway.

Chapter 34

Will was awake early the next morning. He grabbed a cup of coffee and told Hazel he was going out to search again.

"What time will you be back? I have to call the sheriff's office this morning to file a missing person report. I think you should be here for that."

"Okay, you call the sheriff, and I'll be home by noon."

Several officers from the sheriff's department arrived a little before noon, and Will arrived home shortly afterwards. The rest of the afternoon was spent filling out a dozen forms, which included descriptions of Mary, her appearance, clothing she was wearing, the state of her relationship with Will, and any other way Mary could be identified if she was found deceased.

Hazel didn't sleep well that night. Greg was cranky and woke up every hour or so. It was as if he knew something was awry. She loved Greg like he was her own. He was innocent and didn't deserve to be put through all this suffering and grief. It hurt Hazel to watch baby Greg cry for his mother, but all she could do was hold him and try to reassure him that this would all be over soon.

In the morning, members of the sheriff's department, along with the Ventura Police Department, and about 100 volunteers began a massive missing person search. Mary had a lot of friends and family who loved her, and wanted to do everything they could to bring her home safely. Will and all the farm help neglected their work for the following week, so that they could join the search too. Every nook and cranny of Crandall

County was searched. Most places more than once. The entire county was turned upside down. However, the search slowed after three weeks. Not one clue had been found to suggest the whereabouts of Mary Thompson, and the case went cold. Will was considered a suspect for a short time, but law enforcement found no evidence to substantiate the allegations against him. Although he couldn't prove it, Will had suspicions that Mary had been cheating on him and may have run away with her lover. No one, besides Will, believed this, though. People knew Mary as a devoted wife and mother.

Weeks turned into months, and winter arrived. Thanks to Hazel's help, Will stopped running away from his son, and actually started enjoying their time together. Hazel felt a great amount of pride when she saw the two of them together, for she knew she was partially responsible for that. Mary's disappearance was still unexplained, and in a way, acted as the catalyst that brought the three of them together.

The citizens of Ventura did not see things in a good way, though. Rumors began spreading in town that Will got rid of his wife so he could have an affair with the sexy young nanny. These allegations reached the ears of Will, who decided it was best to find a place for Hazel to live. A small cottage on the edge of town became available, so Will rented it for Hazel to live in. It wasn't anything to brag about, but Hazel loved it. A living room, bathroom, bedroom, and eat-in kitchen was all she needed. TJ helped her paint and decorate, and she finally had a place to call home. Will also bought her a beautiful, light blue, 1952 Chevy Belair. That way, Hazel still went to work every day and got paid to be a nanny, but she didn't actually live at Will's.

This arrangement worked well for a few months until one evening in early March 1955. Hazel had had a busy day taking Greg to a doctor's appointment, doing laundry, and cooking dinner for Will. She didn't mind the hard work, she just needed some time to herself. So, after a light supper at home, she turned on the radio, got comfortable on the couch, and opened a new book that she had been dying to read. Unfortunately, she only made it through page three when someone began pounding on her front door.

"Hazel! Open the door, Hazel!" The unmistakable voice of her father, Thomas, was shouting from the other side of the door. She hadn't seen or heard from him since the day she left home, and from the sound of his voice, he had been drinking.

Fear gripped Hazel as she cautiously approached the door. "What do you want, Daddy?"

His tone and manner changed quickly. "I just want to talk with my little girl. Is that okay, baby? Now open the door, so I can see you."

The sound of his voice reminded her of the physical and emotional pain he caused. Her life had changed a great deal since the altercation with her father. She just wanted to be left alone and try to forget about the loss of her baby. Her father, however, had other plans.

"I said open the goddamn door, Hazel! Now!"

Hazel angrily opened the door. "What the hell do you want?" The smell of alcohol filled her nostrils the moment she saw him.

Without an invitation, Thomas pushed her aside and barged into Hazel's living room. "Well, isn't this cozy? The wife is gone, so Will sets up a little love nest where the two of you can play." His insinuating comments angered Hazel, but she was cautious of her words. When Thomas was drinking, his temper was exacerbated.

"It's not like that, Daddy."

"Whatever....I don't care what you do. It's not like you had a great reputation to begin with, anyway. I'm here to make you an offer. If you convince Will to sell his farmland to me, I'll let you back into the family."

Hazel had all she could do to not laugh in his face. "Let me back into the family? Are you serious? I wouldn't come back into your family if you paid me!"

"No, but you sleep with Will Thompson if he pays you."

Without considering her actions, Hazel wound up and with all her might, slapped her father across the cheek. Before her hand returned to her side, Thomas clenched his fist and punched her squarely in the nose. After briefly blacking out, she opened her eyes to discover she was on her knees and a small red puddle of blood had collected in front of her. Slowly getting back to her feet, she swished a mixture of saliva and blood in her mouth and spat it into her father's face. Thomas used his sleeve to wipe his eyes.

"You'll be sorry you ever laid a hand on me," said Thomas as he stormed out.

With blood still dripping from her face, Hazel whispered, "No Daddy, you're going to be the sorry one."

Chapter 35

Tina parked her car and ran in my direction. I didn't know if I should run towards her, or away from her. Seeing her hair blowing in the breeze and knowing what she had, or didn't have, on under her skirt made me want her. On the other hand, I remember what Spirit told me to do....Seek the truth! As we entered my apartment, she turned, and embracing me, asked why I left her office in such a hurry.

"Tina, I'm sorry, but I can't explain it. All I can tell you is that Spirit spoke to me, telling me to go home and seek the truth."

"Seek the truth? You don't believe that I've been telling you the truth?"

"I don't know what to believe. I *can* tell you, though, that your mediumship isn't giving me the answers that I need. I'm sorry, I don't mean to be rude and I appreciate everything you've done for me, but I think I need to see a different medium. At least for a little while, anyway."

With a look of concern on her face, Tina bit her lower lip and said, "That's fine, Jay. If you need to see another medium, I can understand that. I just don't want to lose you."

After assuring her that everything else was fine between us, she pulled me closer and kissed me. I still wasn't sure if I could trust her, but at least things seemed more relaxed now.

"Look, Tina....I drank a few glasses of wine when I got home, and I'm a bit tipsy right now. I'll be the first to admit that I can't hold my liquor, and it doesn't take much to get me drunk. So, I think it would be best if I went to bed."

With a devious grin on her face, Tina unabashedly replied,

"That sounds like a good idea." As she began unbuttoning her blouse, she added, "I think I'll join you!"

"Tina, wait. I don't…." She didn't let me finish.

"Come on Baby. You're not going to turn me down again, are you?" Pulling me closer, she began kissing my neck, and before I knew what was happening, she had maneuvered me into the bedroom. When she unbuckled her belt, her skirt fell to the floor, and I got a good look at the sexiest legs I've ever seen, wrapped in stockings and garters. But she definitely was not wearing panties.

Everything that happened after that was a little fuzzy as the alcohol took over. I vaguely remember losing my pants and falling backwards onto the bed. When Tina climbed on top of me, I tried to reach for a condom, but she pushed me back down and said we didn't need one. She had a contraceptive implant in her arm, so I relaxed and tried to enjoy the ride. Unfortunately, that was about the time that I blacked out. I don't remember what happened after that.

The next morning, I woke up with the worst hangover I've ever had. Tina was already awake and had the ibuprofen and a cup of black coffee waiting for me on the nightstand.

"How long have you been awake?" I asked.

"Just a few minutes. Did you sleep well?"

"Yes, I did."

"So, did you enjoy last night?"

I didn't want to hurt her feelings, so I had to lie. "It was incredible, Baby!"

Tina stared at me for a moment and then broke down in laughter as she admitted nothing had happened between us. "You passed out the moment you hit the bed!"

Feeling embarrassed, I apologized over and over, but Tina didn't seem to mind. "Don't worry about it. We have all day to make up for it."

Tina climbed on top of me, and my headache improved immediately. This was the moment I had been waiting for. The moment I had been fantasizing about. The first time we had sex that morning, it was over very quickly. I couldn't control myself, and neither could she. After a few minutes, we were ready for round two, which lasted much longer. Rounds three and four came later that afternoon, and they were awesome as well. Finally, Tina cried Uncle. She was too sore to go again. I must say that I was proud of myself. I had never gone four times in one day. That was a record for me. So was the number of positions we tried. I would venture to say that it was one of the best days of my life.

After a quick nap, I awoke to see Tina getting dressed. "Are you leaving?" I asked.

"Yes, I have to get going." The tone of her voice was cold.

"Okay. When will I see you again?"

"I really can't say."

Wow, her entire attitude had changed. I didn't understand why she was being so callous.

"I just hope I'm not pregnant."

"But last night you told me you had a contraceptive implant."

"I never said that. You were so drunk last night, I'm surprised you can remember anything."

I think my jaw hit the floor. Tina's attitude had changed completely. Where was this coming from? Yeah, I was drunk last night, but I know what I heard. I've always been extremely careful about using protection.

"So why didn't you say something? I could have used a condom."

"You didn't give me a chance. You were like a crazed animal."

"Tina, what are you talking about? You wanted it as much as I did." I couldn't believe she was acting this way and calling me those names.

"Yeah, if you say so. I have to go...see you around." She stormed out and slammed the door behind her.

My entire world had just come crashing down. The girl of my dreams had just used me and threw me to the curb. And I had no idea why.

Chapter 36

"What do you think you're doing?" asked Will.

Hazel was attempting to pry open Will's gun cabinet with a screwdriver, but she wasn't having any luck doing so. The cabinet remained securely locked. When Hazel turned to look at Will, the bruises on her face were plain as day. The black eye and swollen nose angered Will. He knew the kindness in her heart, and couldn't imagine who would want to hurt her this way.

"Hazel, what happened? Who did this to you?"

She could no longer hold back the tears and began sobbing uncontrollably. "Don't worry about it, Will. I'll take care of it."

"Did your father do this to you?" It became increasingly obvious that his first guess was correct.

"Please, just let me use one of your guns. I'll bring it back in an hour...I promise!"

"No Hazel! It's not worth it. You have your whole life ahead of you. Greg needs you, and so do I."

Will took her in his arms and held her tightly. They stood embracing for several moments until Hazel finally stopped crying. When they gazed into each other's eyes, they could no longer fight the attraction, and gently kissed on the lips. After realizing what had just happened, they both pulled away and apologized. No apologies were necessary, though, for they actually had no regrets.

"Let me take care of it, Hazel."

"No! He's a dangerous man. I don't want you to get hurt. This is my battle...please let me fight it."

"So, you're going to take one of my guns, shoot your old man, and wind up in jail for the rest of your life? What will that accomplish? He'll still come out the winner."

"But what's the difference if you go to him? The result will be the same, and it will be you in jail instead of me."

"No, Hazel. I'll just go talk with him, that's all."

"Talk with my father? Are you serious? There's no talking with my father, especially if he's been drinking."

"It'll be fine, you'll see."

Will got in his truck and drove away. Hazel tried to say a prayer, but she was shaking so badly, the words wouldn't come out. Staying busy was the only thing that would get her through this day, so she woke Greg and prepared his breakfast. Greg resembled Will in many ways. High cheekbones and a cleft chin made them both look distinguished. He also shared some features with Mary, but they never discussed them. Will still believed that Mary ran away with her lover, and would almost assuredly return one day to claim custody of her son. As for Hazel, she couldn't believe a mother would voluntarily walk away from her child. Kidnapping and/or murder was her guess as to why Mary disappeared. At this point, though, it would be awkward if Mary came home. Romantic feelings between her and Will was the last thing she was expecting, but it felt nice. It made her feel like a schoolgirl. She just feared that her father would steal her happiness again.

After breakfast, she put Greg in his playpen, washed the dishes, and did a load of laundry. She worked extra fast that morning, so she could have Will's lunch on the table at noon. The lunch hour, however, came and went, and Will never showed. Hazel fed Greg at 1:00pm, and afterwards laid him down for a nap. Pacing back and forth in front of the living room bay window, she had a good view of the driveway, and would know when Will arrived.

Greg awoke from his nap at 2:30pm, so Hazel filled his tub and bathed him. After he was clean and dried, Hazel dressed him in the cutest little outfit of a flannel shirt and bib overalls, which she had purchased at Sears & Roebuck. Grabbing a few of his favorite toys, she sat next to him on the floor and played with him. Finally, at 4:15, the front door opened, and Will strolled in, looking triumphant.

"Oh my God, are you okay? I was so worried about you!" cried Hazel.

"Yep, everything is fine! I told you it would be."

"So, did you speak with him?"

"Briefly. He was busy working on one of his old John Deere tractors. I just told him to stay away from you. He won't be bothering you again."

"Will, you don't know my father. How can you be so sure about this?"

Will moved close to her and stared deeply into her eyes. "Hazel, believe me when I tell you he will never, ever bother you again."

With that remark, Hazel knew that something bad had happened. Something terrible. But she also knew that her father deserved whatever happened to him. And she made a promise to herself that she would never question Will about what had happened that day.

Hazel returned home at 7:00 that evening. It had been a long day, and she was looking forward to a hot bath and some quiet reading time. Her plans would have to be put on hold though, for when she turned into her driveway, TJ's pickup truck was there. TJ was seated on her front steps. After parking her car, TJ approached her. She could see the look of concern on his face.

"He's gone, Sis. He's really gone."

"What are you talking about? Who's gone?"

"Dad...he's dead."

Hazel felt a chill go down her spine. She knew something bad had happened, but reality hadn't set in until now. "How did it happen?" Hazel asked, but wasn't sure if she wanted to know the answer to that question.

"He was working underneath a tractor. The jack stand broke, and it came down on top of him."

Hazel felt relieved. She felt no remorse, no sadness, and no guilt. Only relief. Thomas got what he deserved, and there were no suspicious circumstances. "Oh TJ, I'm so sorry. I know how much you loved him."

"Loved him? You think I loved him? I hated his guts. You think you were the only one he beat? He beat me every time I made a mistake on the farm. No matter how small."

"But why didn't you leave? You didn't have to take that abuse."

"I had nowhere else to go. Besides, I knew I was the sole heir to the farm, the house, the money....everything. I knew if I waited long enough, it would all be mine."

Hazel felt relieved that it was over, but she felt a bit jealous that TJ would get everything. She knew nothing about farming, and the house held too many terrible memories. But she could surely use some cash. Will had provided her with a place to live and a car, but a little extra spending money would be nice.

There was no funeral. Thomas didn't have any friends, just business associates. For many residents of Crandall County, it was actually good riddance. The mood on the farm was greatly improved, for none of the employees cared for Thomas. They had been there for the money, nothing more. The reading of the will was held two weeks later. Hazel attended, only to be supportive of TJ. Dark and smoky were the only words that could describe the office of Harold Thorndyke, the Bowen family attorney. Harold was 78 years old and had been semi-retired for several years. Thomas was his last client, and Harold had only continued to represent him because of the pay.

Hazel actually felt a little sad about the proceedings. A man who was very successful in his life, but alienated all of his friends and family. Now only three people were left to close out his financial affairs. Thorndyke wasted little time reading the will.

"I, Thomas Bowen, being of sound mind and body, leave $500,000 cash to my daughter Hazel. The remainder of my assets, including cash, house, farm, vehicles, and any additional possessions, shall all go to my son, Thomas Jr."

Hazel was in shock. She hadn't been expecting anything. TJ was ecstatic with the results, as he gave Hazel a big hug.

"I'm so glad that he remembered you in his will! You deserve this for all the bullshit you put up with. Now you can make a fresh start."

Hazel considered TJ's words for a moment. *A fresh start.* Those words created so many ideas in her mind. She could move to Chicago, buy a big house, a new car, maybe go back to college, maybe even start her own business. Opening a childcare center, or maybe even a preschool, had always enticed her. But these thoughts didn't last long. She quickly realized that she was where she wanted to be. She loved her life. She loved Greg and Will and her little house and her car. And now, there would be no one who would want to take that away from her. Hazel knew now she could finally be happy.

Chapter 37

"Here you are, Mr. Thompson," said Patty as she handed me a large manila envelope.

Mister. I was really beginning to hate that word.

"Your title and all applicable paperwork for the property at 277 Roberts Road are enclosed in this envelope."

"You mean it's mine? It's really mine?"

"Yep. Lock, stock, and barrel. Congratulations, it's all yours!"

"I still don't understand how. I've paid no taxes on it."

"Well, someone has." Patty got up from her desk and opened a file cabinet drawer.

I shook my head in disbelief. "But who?"

"I have no idea." She put duplicates of the paperwork in the drawer and pushed it closed. "Whoever it was, carefully covered their tracks," added Patty.

"So, I can go there and cut the locks off the gates?"

"Yep. But you might want to get Sheriff Booker to go with you."

I remembered what happened as a result of my last visit to Roberts Road. "Good idea!"

*   *   *

"Hold my radio, Jason," said Sheriff Booker. "While I cut this lock off."

Grabbing his radio, I asked, "Sheriff, how long has this fence been here?"

"I can't answer that. It's been here longer than I have. I came to

Ventura with my parents back in '65 and the fence was already here." The sheriff used three foot long bolt cutters and had to use a good amount of muscle to cut the first padlock. As he was unwrapping the chain that was laced through the steel fence and gate, he added, "Oh, and Jason, I'm sorry, but we have made no headway in finding the people who assaulted you. We haven't given up, but so far we're turning up zeroes."

Honestly, I wasn't expecting them to. I didn't give them much to go on.

After opening the first gate, Sheriff Booker turned his attention to the padlock on the hasp holding the wooden gate closed. This one cut much easier. Before opening the gate, he looked at me and asked, "Are you ready?"

I nodded. Actually, I felt like a character in The Secret Garden, expecting to go from a mundane exterior to a beautiful, extraordinarily colorful world of flowers, ponds, and butterflies. You can imagine my disappointment when the gate swung open, and all I could see were trees, shrubs, and weeds overgrown to the point, it resembled a jungle. The vegetation was so dense, you could barely see through it, much less walk through.

"Holy shit," said Sheriff Booker.

I remained silent, for there was nothing more I could add to that statement. Just to our right, though, there was a pathway. It was wide enough to drive a car through and extended through the brush further than we could see. Rather than taking a chance of getting our cars stuck in the mud, we decided to walk along the pathway. Not knowing what or whom we might meet up with, I stayed close to the sheriff. At least he was armed.

At roughly seventy-five feet in, we came upon a clearing. There was no way to prepare myself for what was there, for in the center of that clearing stood a house. Not just any old house, but a large farmhouse. You would think that a farmhouse in this dense jungle would be in a rundown condition, but this was not the case. This was a magnificent house, with white clapboard siding, black shutters, a gray shingled roof, and a grand wraparound porch. This all added up to a farmhouse that looked completely out of place against its surroundings.

"Holy shit." The sheriff said it again.

Again, I was speechless. This had to have been Caleb and Flora's house. This was, after all, The Thompson Family Farm. At least it used to be. I know that Grandpa Will continued to farm this land after his parents had passed, but according to my records, he didn't live here. He had his own house on the other side of town. But who had been taking care of it? This house was in pristine condition. None of this made any sense.

"Sheriff, since I own the land, does it mean that I also own the house?"

"Yes, sir. It's all yours."

"Holy shit," I replied.

"My thoughts exactly," added the sheriff.

After doing a quick walk-around of the exterior, I asked Sheriff Booker if he wanted to see the inside.

"Hell yeah, I do."

It was an easy entrance, as the front door was unlocked. I entered cautiously, afraid of who might be waiting for us inside. The sheriff followed closely behind me, with one hand on his firearm. When we stepped inside, I was astonished. The interior of the house appeared to be brand new. Fresh paint on the walls, bead board ceilings, hardwood floors, and all new appliances in the kitchen. This was really unbelievable. There was no way this house had been vacant. People had been living there, and it had been recent. There was an abundance of dust bunnies on the floor, which made it obvious that all the furniture had been abruptly removed.

The upstairs was equally impressive. Fabric wallpaper, modern windows, and wall to wall carpeting gave it a cozy feeling. It was all so beautiful, but also so confusing. Who had been living here, and who had spent so much money on a house they didn't own? And why this house? Why would anyone want to spend a boatload of money on a house sitting in the middle of a jungle?

"So what do you think , Sheriff?"

"I think I have to get back to the courthouse," said Sheriff Booker, as he shook my hand.

"You're leaving?"

"Yep. I have to go do my job and fight crime. Don't worry though, I'm just a phone call away."

The Sheriff walked towards Roberts Road and I realized what a desolate place this was. Actually, it was only about five miles from town as the crow flies, but it felt so much further because of the tangled vegetation. While I continued to search the interior, the unmistakable sound of tires crunching on gravel echoed through the air. Maybe Sheriff Booker forgot something? Or maybe it was the men who assaulted me, and they had come back to finish the job they started. I didn't want to stick around to find out. I ran out the back door, jumped off the porch, and ducked behind a lilac bush. The car stopped just shy of the house, so I couldn't get a good look at it. Reaching around on the ground, I found a good-sized branch. At least this time I would have a weapon. As the car door swung open, the crisp sound of leaves rustling filled the air. This was the sound of footsteps, and they were coming closer.

Suddenly, a voice said, "Jason! Jason Thompson! Get your ass out here, now!"

Chapter 38

TJ Bowen took a long drag from his cigar. Not just any cigar, mind you, but a cigar that he had imported from Cuba, selling for $400 per box. He had on his best Stetson hat, and a pair of $800 western boots. Strutting through the fields of The Thompson Family Farm, his chest out and his head held high, he was proud of what he had. And what he had become. In all honesty, he had become his father. For as much as he hated his father, he was now a mirror image of him. TJ's love of money and material possessions sometimes made him worse than his father.

Will Thompson was gone and would no longer get in his way. Will had left his house and some cash to Hazel, but the farm was not included in the will. TJ was in control of these fields now, and would become the owner as soon as he could manipulate the law in his favor.

It was not an easy time for Hazel. Although she and Will never wed, he was the love of her life. He was the only man to give her the love and respect she deserved. A heart attack was the apparent cause of his death, even though he appeared to be in perfect health. Besides the house and money, he left two more gifts for Hazel. One was a son, David, whom she loved with all her heart. The other was the custodianship of Greg, whom she loved like he was her own. She couldn't give David the Thompson surname, and she refused to give him the Bowen moniker, so she gave him her mother's maiden name, White.

TJ would go on to marry Kate Jefferson, the most beautiful woman in Ventura. The marriage was a sham right from the start. TJ wanted a trophy wife, and Kate was known in Crandall County as a gold digger. They had one child together, James Bowen. All outward appearances would suggest that they were a happy couple and had a grand marriage. In reality, Kate stuck it out for twenty years, and then filed for divorce. The constant mental and physical abuse she received from TJ was too much for her to bear. In the divorce papers, Kate was asking for the house, and half of everything else they had. After reading these papers, TJ tore them up and threw them in the trash. Shortly after that, Kate disappeared and was never heard from again.

TJ and Hazel had grown distant. After thinking things over, he didn't believe that Hazel deserved her inheritance money. Why should she receive a half million dollars from a father she hated? Dad must have forgotten to change the will. That's the only explanation that TJ could think of. Hazel kept her distance from him though, for every time she looked at TJ, she saw her father. The memories were so painful; it was easier to just stay away from him.

Things were changing in Crandall County. Farming was not as profitable as it once was, and more and more farmers were finding easier ways to make a living. By 1965, TJ had had enough and called it quits. He sold his land to developers who wanted it to build middle class housing developments. Besides, he had other fish to fry, which were much more profitable. His actions, however, were very secretive. As his son, James, grew, the two of them became thick as thieves, always scheming ways to increase the family fortune.

When David White graduated from Ventura High School in 1975, his goal was to attend the University of Illinois, and become an elementary school teacher. Be that as it may, he changed his mind when he discovered it would require six years of college. David wasn't willing to sacrifice six years of his life for a career he wasn't sure he would enjoy. So, he settled for a job as a teacher's assistant at his mother's pre-school. Actually, it angered David to have to work every day. He was lazy and felt that he deserved some of the Bowen family fortune. Hazel had taken her inheritance and made some wise investments with it. In 15 years, she had doubled her money. David didn't understand why either of them had to work.

Greg, meanwhile, grew up with a love of cars and trucks. During his junior year at Ventura High, he began attending tech school. Two years of studies taught him the basics of auto repair, and with a loan from Hazel, he was able to start his own business. Greg proved he was a natural, and his reputation as the best auto mechanic around quickly spread throughout the county. Soon, people were coming from miles away to have Greg work on their vehicles. Within a year, he made enough money to repay Hazel's loan with interest. This made her extremely proud of him, and she knew Will would feel the same if he could see him.

David, on the other hand, continued to work at the pre-school with no real ambition in life. He was content to live a life of nonchalance, believing that someday he would be the heir to his mother's money.

The only thing that Greg and David had in common was they both married, and started families, at roughly the same time. Greg's firstborn was a boy, Jason Thompson. David's first was a girl, Tina White.

Chapter 39

"Jason, can you hear me?"

I knew that voice. "Sue! Is that you?"

"Yeah, it's me. Who'd you think it was?"

I crawled out of the brush and dropped the stick I was holding.

Sue laughed when she saw me. "What are you gonna do, beat me up?"

I ran over and gave her a hug. Hugs from Sue were awesome. She didn't have a great body, but it just felt right to hold her in my arms...even if it was just for a moment. She had obviously come on her lunch break, for she was wearing a dark green dress which contrasted nicely with her auburn hair. "What are you doing here?" I asked.

"I was curious. Heard you're a proud new homeowner and thought I'd come check out your new place."

"Boy, news spreads fast in this town."

"Yes, it does. So, are you going to give me the ten cent tour?"

"Sure, come with me," I said as I grabbed her hand.

We did a quick walk-around of the exterior and then headed inside.

Walking through each room of the house was thoroughly enjoyable. It was the first time since graduation that Sue and I had spent more than just a few minutes together. Chatting while strolling from room to room brought back so many memories from when we were young. After walking through the entire house, Sue paused and smiled at me. Neither of us had realized that we were still holding hands.

"Jay, it's beautiful, but what the hell is a house like this doing in the middle of a jungle?"

"I'm pretty sure this was my great-grandparents' house, and at one time, this was their farm. I don't have a clue what happened here since then."

"So, what are you going to do here? I mean, are you planning on living here?"

"I don't know. I'm not sure what I want to do yet."

Sue still hadn't let go of my hand. I wasn't complaining.

"Jay, where's your girlfriend?"

"Which one?" I asked.

"I don't know...pick one."

"Well, I'm thinking that I'm single again. I broke up with Lisa because she was cheating on me. And I assume Tina broke up with me. I haven't heard from her in three weeks. She moved out of her office *and* her apartment, and she won't return my phone calls."

"Wow, that didn't last long."

"Yeah, I don't get it."

"I'm sorry, Jay. You don't need this shit. You deserve to be happy."

"You do too, Sue." I knew she had gone through a very rough spell after her divorce. "Maybe we acted too harshly back in high school. Maybe we shouldn't have given up after just one date."

"Hey, it's never too late. Maybe we should try again?" Sue replied.

One more hug, but this time I didn't want to let go.

*   *   *

After stopping and picking up a pizza for dinner, I arrived home to my apartment at 6:30pm. An unfamiliar car was parked in my driveway, and it immediately brought back memories of being assaulted. I didn't want to go through that again, especially since all of my wounds had finally healed. It was a pleasant surprise, however. The car belonged to my favorite medium, Amber Crystal.

I parked my car, grabbed my pizza, and walked toward my apartment door. Amber waddled along behind me.

"Excuse me, sir!" she yelled out to me. "It's me, Amber Crystal. Do you remember me?"

First medium that I ever really trusted. But she was strange... very strange.

"Of course I remember you! Come inside and have some pizza with me, ok?"

Her face and all of her freckles lit up like a Christmas tree. "Yes, sir, Mister Thompson, right behind you!"

Mister!...I hate that word.

Once inside, I grabbed some plates and napkins. "Have a seat, Amber. You want something to drink? All I have is ginger ale." I pulled out a kitchen chair and cleared a spot on the table for her plate.

"Yes, sir, ginger ale is fine. But I have something very important to discuss with you." This time she had on a lime green maxi-dress with green and white striped crocs.

"Okay, we can talk while we eat our pizza."

I poured two glasses of ginger ale and put slices of pizza on each of our plates. It was okay. Not as good as Tony's, but it would do in a pinch.

"So, Mr. Thompson..."

"Please! Call me Jason. Or Jay. Just don't call me Mister, okay?"

"Yes sir! Sorry about that. So, as I was saying, I have been receiving a lot of messages from the spirit world. Most of these messages are coming from your family."

"Really?" I asked. Actually, I wanted to have some fun and test her to see if she was being truthful. "Which family members have been contacting you?"

"Caleb, Flora, Mary, and Greg."

"And how are these people related to me?" Anyone could look up ancestors on the internet.

"You don't know these people?" she asked.

"Oh, I know who these people are. I just want to see if you do."

"Ahh, I get it. You're testing me. Okay, Caleb and Flora are your great-grandparents, Mary is your grandmother, and Greg is your father. Do I pass?"

"Umm…yeah. So, what have they been saying to you?"

"Well, they've been speaking so quickly, it's been difficult to understand what they're trying to say. I'm clairvoyant, but my clairaudience needs some work, so I don't always catch everything that comes through. What I have been able to interpret, though, is they have been trying to contact you, but something or someone has been blocking their communication. They all fear for your safety, and want to warn you of a person or persons who mean you harm, and will stop at nothing to get what they want."

Come to think of it, I have had no visits from any spirits recently."Who is this person?" I asked.

"They're not saying any names, but I'm sensing that it's someone close to you."

I thought about it for a moment, but couldn't think of anyone. In fact, everyone who had been close to me had recently abandoned me. Lisa, Kyle, Tina…people I thought I could trust, but obviously couldn't. Sue is the only friend I have left. And, with a chance of us rekindling feelings from the past, I refuse to believe that she would want to hurt me. Still, it's probably best to keep my guard up.

"Mister…oops, I mean Jason, did you say you had been getting readings from another medium?"

"Yes…well, she *called* herself a medium, anyway."

"I see. I just thought maybe she could help us interpret the messages from your family. Can I ask what her name is?"

"Her name is Tina White," I replied.

A look of fear flashed over Amber's face. Not knowing if she was feeling anger or pity, she reached for my hand and squeezed it tightly.

"Jason, stay away from that woman. Stay far away from her. I don't know what she is, but she is definitely not a medium. She has never done any good, and usually creates havoc in the spirit world."

"Havoc in the spirit world? How does she do that?"

Still squeezing my hand, she replied, "Spirits have lived their lives on earth, some good, some not so good. But they all deserve to rest in peace. Tina White doesn't allow this to happen. She uses the spirit world to come between families who are mourning."

"But why would she do such a terrible thing?"

"I'm not sure, but money is usually involved. She and her whacko husband are money hungry thieves."

I sat there, staring at Amber, feeling an anxiety attack coming on. I could literally feel my brain spinning inside my skull. Feeling dizzy, I put my head down on the kitchen table, hoping that the world would stop spinning.

"Jason, what's wrong? Are you okay?"

Amber stood next to me, rubbing my back, trying to get me to speak. It took nearly two minutes for the spinning to cease. Slowly, I raised my head and focused on Amber's face. Struggling to get the words out, I murmured, "Did you say husband?"

"Yes, he claims to be a therapist, but he's crazier than his patients!"

"What is his name?" I asked, but dreading her reply.

"Phillips, I think. Kenneth Phillips."

The spinning started again, only worse.

Chapter 40

"Jay, why are you telling me all of this?" asked Sue. "It's none of my business."

I had brought sandwiches and chips to surprise her, so we could have lunch together on one of the picnic tables outside the courthouse. However, I could sense that she was getting upset.

"But it is your business. I want you to know what's going on in my life."

"Do you really have to tell me how many times you had unprotected sex with a married woman? I don't think I need to know that."

"Sue, I was drunk. She didn't tell me she was married. And, I'm positive she told me she had a birth control implant. The next day she was practically blaming me for getting her pregnant, and then she disappeared. I'm not proud of what I've done, but I want to be totally honest with you."

"Okay, now can we just drop it?"

"I'm sorry Sue, I don't mean to make you mad."

"I'm not mad, I'm just..."

"Jealous?" I asked.

Our eyes met, and it sent a warm feeling through my whole body. "Maybe a little," she replied.

"Don't be. I've learned my lesson. You can trust me."

"I hope so."

It had been two years since her divorce. She and Bob seemed like the perfect couple, always laughing and joking. Sue had wanted to start a family, and she thought Bob did too. When she got pregnant, she broke the news to him over a romantic, candlelit dinner. Bob didn't share her enthusiasm, though, as he pulled the rug out from under her. He packed his bags and left the next day. Sue miscarried two months later, buried herself in her job, and had yet to crawl out from under the memories.

"So, you're really jealous?" I asked.

"Don't let it go to your head. It's not like I want to have unprotected sex with you."

Sue grinned at me, and I burst out laughing.

"Have you spoken with Dr. Phillips?"

"No, and I don't plan on it. If he doesn't know about his wife, then I don't want to be the one to tell him. If he does know, well, that's just plain weird."

"So, what are you going to do if she's pregnant?"

"I'll cross that bridge when I come to it."

Honestly, I hadn't even considered that scenario. I couldn't afford to take care of myself. How was I supposed to take care of a child?

"Sue, my life is a train wreck. If you want to bail out now, I'll understand."

"Shut up, Jay. We walked away from each other a long time ago. Let's not do it again."

I like the way she thinks.

*   *   *

"Well?"

"Well, what?" Tina replied.

"Are you?" asked Ken Phillips.

There was only one pink line in the result window.

"No, damn it! He must shoot blanks. We did it four times."

"You could go back and try again."

"No way. I will not let him or any other guy cum inside me again. It makes me feel so dirty." Tina was adamant about her feelings.

"Okay, don't get upset. You're not pregnant, but he doesn't

know that. Tell him you are and see where it goes."

"Alright, Baby. We'll give it a shot."

Chapter 41

"What do you want, Lisa?"

James Bowen was rude to his daughter because she was no longer useful to him.

"I came to say goodbye, Daddy," Lisa spoke quietly, as she slowly walked into his office.

He lowered his eyeglasses down to the tip of his nose so that he could peer over them.

"Goodbye? Are you going somewhere?"

"I'm moving. There's nothing left for me here." Lisa struggled to fight back the tears that were filling her eyes.

"Well, maybe if you had done what I asked, things would have worked out fine."

"I'm sorry, Daddy. I tried, I really tried."

"You obviously didn't try hard enough!" James raised his voice. "So, you screw things up here, then decide to run away and make a fresh start? That takes a hell of a lot of nerve."

Lisa felt so much resentment towards her father, but decided it was best to bite her tongue. She wouldn't take another undeserved beating from him.

"There's still time for you to try one more time," James added. "All you have to do is act like a slut. That should be easy for you."

It was at that moment, that very moment, everything in Lisa's brain went numb. The pain was gone; the sadness was gone; the joy was gone, and the tears in her eyes dried up. The memories of mental, physical, and sexual abuse her father had imposed on her were still there. But it didn't matter anymore, for she couldn't feel them. It was as if her mind had been paused. She had spent all her days trying to bring some happiness to the men in her life. It obviously didn't make a difference. No one should ever have to feel used and abused, especially from their own father, but Lisa had. Jason was the only man she knew who had never hurt her. But she royally screwed that up.

She turned and walked away from her father without uttering another word. James continued to berate his daughter as she left, but she wasn't listening. It didn't matter anymore. She felt nothing.

*   *   *

"What can I do for you, Sheriff?" asked Kyle Butler.

Sheriff Booker entered the dispatch office of Butler Transportation, had a look around, and had a seat on Jason's old desk top.

"For starters, you can pour me a cup of coffee."

"Sure Sheriff, how do you take it?"

"Black, no sugar. Mr. Butler, have you heard that your former employee, Jason Thompson, has learned that he is the owner of some land on Roberts Road?"

"I heard that."

"So, you're aware of what might happen to anyone who has known the truth about that land? Or should I say anyone who has known the truth but chose to keep it concealed?"

"Why are you telling me this?" asked Kyle.

"Don't play dumb with me. I know you're screwing his old lady. Hell, half the county knows that. What I don't know is what you two have been scheming."

"Nothing, Sheriff. I swear."

"Good. Let's keep it that way." Sheriff Booker took one last gulp of his coffee and added, " Oh, and Mr. Butler...if anything should happen to Jason, the first person I would apprehend would be you. Have I made myself clear, Mr. Butler?"

"Perfectly."

Sheriff Booker made similar visits that day, to the office of

Dr. Ken Phillips and to Tony Rienzi's Italian Restaurant. The conversations and warnings were almost identical to the one he had with Kyle Butler. The Sheriff was no angel, and God knows he profited from his knowledge and his ability to look the other way. However, he could no longer ignore the guilt that had been building up inside his mind. Jason Thompson was a man who had lost his entire family. The women he thought he could trust had used him. Perhaps he was naïve, unable to see the forest through the trees, but he did nothing to deserve the treatment he had received. His only guilt was being a Thompson. It was time for Sheriff Booker to assist Jason in evening the score.

Chapter 42

"Come on, lazy!" shouted Sue. "You still have five more boxes to bring in."

Attempting to cut my losses, Sue had been helping me move everything from my apartment to the house. I couldn't afford to keep both. If I didn't do something soon, though, I would be forced to sell. For the first time in my life, I was broke, and I had maxed out my credit cards. None of the local banks would give me a loan, and I can't say that I blame them. Maybe I could eat some crow and ask Kyle for my job back? Nope, not unless I'm desperate!

"No fair, you moved all the light boxes and left the heavy ones for me."

"Well, of course, I'm not stupid!"

Sue was a good friend. I hadn't realized how much I had missed spending time with her. The past couple of weeks had given us a chance to catch up and become reacquainted with each other. I still hadn't kissed her, but that would come in time. I hope. For now, I only wanted to prove that she could trust me.

The moving van brought my furniture at 3:00pm, and in the meantime, she and I continued to unpack. We had everything finished by 5:00pm and started feeling the pangs of hunger. Sue grabbed my hand and said, "Come on Turkey, let's go to the diner for some dinner. You drive and I'll buy." She had many nicknames for me, but 'Turkey' was one of her favorites.

"Sue, I appreciate everything you've done for me, but I can't keep accepting gifts like that."

"Sure you can. You forget how well I know you. As soon as

you get back on your feet, you'll repay every one of those favors. I know you will. I'm starving, so let's go get something to eat, okay?"

"You're the best, Sue. Thank you."

We got in my car, but wouldn't you know, it wouldn't start. Petey was getting old, but I was in no shape financially to buy a new car. I had no other choice but to ride with Sue. She had a brand new SUV, black with silver trim. I don't even know the make or model, but it was nice…very nice.

The Ventura Diner was extremely busy, as it usually is every day around dinner time. As we entered, Gloria Ferguson handed menus to us and told us to sit wherever we'd like. She gave me an odd glance as I walked past her. It was obvious she remembered the last time I was there.

We sat at a booth near the jukebox, and Sue whispered, "Why is she looking at you like that?"

I chuckled, "You don't want to know." So far, I had only seen living customers in the diner. I wanted to tell her everything about my family, and the spirits I had been seeing, but it would have to wait until we were alone and I had plenty of time to explain.

The 'Happy Waitress' seemed like the perfect item to order. It was filling, delicious, and cheap. I didn't want Sue spending a lot of money on me.

"Jay, I might be able to get you a job with the county. You know, maybe with the sanitation department, or you could learn to become a court transcriber. There are always jobs available with Crandall County. Jay, are you listening to me? Jay?"

It was happening again. This time, a dark shadow was hovering about five feet away from our table. I rubbed my eyes and tried to get a clearer view. The shadow's features became sharper, and soon I was aware it was my father, Greg Thompson. My dad was the greatest man I ever met. He was smart, talented, and loving. He was also the best father a boy could ever ask for. As he came closer, my heart raced. I could hear no words, yet his thoughts were being etched on my mind. I understood what he was trying to communicate.

"Be prepared for something big. We will be there for you," was all I could make out, but that was more than enough. The image only lasted a few seconds, but it was one that I would never forget. And it was becoming more and more obvious that I didn't need a medium in my life. My spiritual abilities were becoming stronger, and communication with the spirit world was becoming easier.

"Hey, Turkey! What the hell is wrong with you?"

I snapped out of it and realized that Sue was speaking to me. Maybe it was a coincidence, but I'm pretty sure Lisa said those same words to me the last time I was here.

"I'm sorry, Sue. I had something on my mind."

"Yeah, probably thinking about married women," she said with a grin on her face.

"Nope, just thinking about the beautiful woman sitting across from me."

"Yeah, right. Nice try, Jay. But still…that was the first time you ever called me beautiful."

I reached for Sue's hand and said, "I should have said that to you a long time ago. I have always thought of you as a good friend, but just recently I've discovered that you're much more than that."

"Thanks Jay. That means a lot to me."

After dinner, Sue asked if I'd like to go to her place to watch a movie. I declined the invitation, though. It was getting late and there were many things I wanted to accomplish at my house the next day. When she dropped me off, it was very difficult to say goodnight. We sat in her car for a few moments, staring deeply into each other's eyes. I had never felt this close to Sue, and I desperately wanted to touch her physically. Not sex, but just to hold her and kiss her would feel so good. I could sense that she wanted it too, but I was so afraid of scaring her off. So, I thanked her again and gave her a quick kiss on the cheek as we said goodnight. Knowing that Sue was hurting and cautious made it easier for me to be patient, if that made any sense. One step at a time...there was plenty of time for us.

Chapter 43

L isa Bowen tossed and turned all night long. She desperately needed sleep, but it just wasn't happening. The weight of the world was upon her shoulders, and would stay there until she righted some wrongs. Some of these wrongs were caused by her, others by her family. There were also wrongs caused by a group of selfish men and women who felt the Thompson family owed them. Whatever the cause, and whomever was to blame, Lisa knew she could find no peace in her new life until she corrected the mistakes of the past. Jason appeared to be the victim of all the wickedness in Crandall County, but he was totally oblivious to what was happening right under his nose. He was innocent, and Lisa was the only person who could correct all the mistakes of the past. She, alone, could end the lies, theft, and murders of the past. But, to do so, would mean revealing long kept secrets of the past. She had no other choice, though. It was all or nothing. If she was going to do this, she'd have to go all the way, even if it meant destroying family allegiances.

She was showered and dressed by 6:00am. Wearing a black pinstripe skirt suit with black stockings and heels, Lisa looked like a million bucks. There would be no breakfast this morning, for even the smell of coffee made her nauseous. Lisa felt confident, though. After all these years, she was finally going to stand on her own two feet and do the right thing. Her suitcase had been packed for several days, so she threw it in the trunk of her car, just in case she needed to make a quick getaway. There was just one last item left in the motel room where she had been staying. A small towel rolled into a ball was in the nightstand drawer. She cautiously removed the towel, exposing what had been a twenty-first birthday gift from her father. A Smith & Wesson CSX handgun. Although Lisa had passed her marksmanship classes with flying colors and held her concealed carry permit for nearly nine years, she rarely took the pistol out of the house. Today was an exception, though. She wanted to keep it close today...just in case.

Lisa's first stop that morning was to be at the office of Dr. Ken Phillips. At one time, she was infatuated with Dr. Phillips. Despite his marriage and her engagement, they couldn't resist each other. Their torrid affair, however, fizzled out as quickly as it began. They both shared some knowledge with each other that should have been kept a secret, and opened up a very large can of worms. Now, however, she flinches at the thought of him touching her.

Lisa didn't bother knocking on his office door. Today, she was in control and would pull no punches. Ken seemed a bit startled as Lisa barged in. The grave look on her face showed Ken that this was not a social call, but he had seen this look before and wasn't fearful of Lisa. She had a history of bringing drama to the table, and Ken knew how to deal with it.

"Lisa! Come on in! It's so nice to see you...what can I do for you today?" Ken stood and tried to give her a friendly embrace.

Lisa wasn't impressed. "Cut the crap, Ken," she said as she pushed him away.

"My, aren't we crotchety this morning?"

"Screw you! Sit down and shut up. We need to get some things out in the open."

With the fake smile of a used car salesman, he took a seat behind his desk.

"Okay, Lisa. What *things* are you referring to?"

"As if you didn't know. It's time we come clean and inform Jason of all the wrongdoing that's been occurring for years."

With an arrogant chuckle, Ken replied, "*We*?? Did you say *we*? *You* are the biggest hypocrite and slut in the county. Despite being engaged to Jason, *you* told him more lies than anyone else, and *you* couldn't control your sexual appetite. How many guys have *you* slept with since you've been with Jason? I may have told him a few lies, but I did nothing to hurt him."

"No? How about the beating that you and Tony gave him?"

Ken paused and glared at Lisa. "Don't even start that! You can't prove I was involved in that violence."

"Sheriff Booker told me all about it. And you have some nerve calling me a slut while your wife is sleeping with Jason!"

"You're just jealous, Lisa. Soon, Tina and I will be living on easy street and there's nothing you can do to stop it."

This enraged Lisa. "Don't tell me she really went through with it!"

Ken gave her a cocky smirk as he stood and walked to his office door. "I think it's time for you to leave. We have nothing left to discuss."

Strike one for Lisa. There was no way she was going to win this argument. A deep breath followed by a quick prayer asking for forgiveness was all she needed. Reaching into her purse, she pulled out her handgun and aimed it at Ken's chest.

"Put that away, Lisa, before you hurt yourself!"

A warm smile and a satisfied look came across her face as she squeezed the trigger twice and gazed at the blood pouring out of a rather large hole in his chest. A momentary look of shock appeared on Ken's face when he realized Lisa hadn't been bluffing. It lasted less than a second, though, as all life exited his body. He was dead before he hit the floor.

Happiness filled Lisa's soul. She had never known such joy, for this may have been the first time in her life that she put someone else's feelings ahead of her own. Stepping over Ken's lifeless body, she ran to her car. It was time to move on to her second stop of the morning.

Chapter 44

This was going to take some time to get used to. Waking up in a big house was an awesome feeling, but it was missing something. Specifically, it needed a family. *I need a family.* A wife, a few kids, maybe the in-laws. I tried to picture it in my mind. Sue fit the bill as the wife. She could be a ball-buster at times, but that's one thing I like about her. And I know how much she loves children. She had planned on having a big family with Bob until he bailed on her. Maybe there's a future for the Thompson family? Woah, things were going way too fast, and anxiety was kicking into high gear. I wasn't sure exactly how Sue felt about me, and I didn't even have a job. One step at a time. The first thing I wanted to do was explore the rest of my property. Well, actually the second thing. First thing was coffee, then I would explore.

I found the oldest jeans and hoodie that I owned and got dressed. The only boots I had were winter boots, but they served the purpose. I filled a travel mug with coffee and set out on foot. It was a beautiful morning for a walk. I only wish more of the sun and sky were visible. The trees and brush were so thick, it could have passed for dusk.

The cleared path coming in from Roberts Road didn't end at my house. It continued on through the woods, so that's where I was headed. Normally, I steer clear of the woods. You never know who or what you'll meet up with. But this was different. These were *my* woods, on *my* property, and there had been a huge fence surrounding the land for a long time. No chance for any enormous animals to come in. As I strolled along the pathway, I could see tire tracks in the dried mud. These weren't the imprints of a car tire, though. They were wide and had an all-terrain type of tread. Something that a tractor or large truck would have. Off to my right was an old farm tractor. There was no paint left on it because it was completely rusted. From the looks of it, the old tractor hadn't been moved in many years. The tracks definitely had not been made by this tractor.

After walking about a quarter mile, I came to a large clearing. It measured roughly one hundred yards by one hundred yards. Trees, shrubs, bushes, ivy...everything had been cleared from the land. Along the edge of the clearing, rotting logs were strewn on the ground. The trees here were obviously cut down many years ago. The most noticeable detail, though, was the lack of grass. This was freshly dug soil, loose and not compacted. Someone had been digging here recently, but for what?

Suddenly, my name was being called. Not the type of calling from someone in close proximity, but a strong echo was noticeable. It was as if someone at the end of a long hallway was trying to get my attention. The hazy outline of a man stood on the opposite side of the clearing. As I approached, I could sense that this was the person or spirit who had been calling me. With caution, I moved closer towards the mysterious figure. I said a brief prayer asking my spirit guide to help me communicate, as I spoke my first words.

"Who is there? Please make yourself known."

I felt the spirit reply, not with words, but his thoughts were etched into my mind.

"Jason, let go of this place. Turn and run far away, and never look back."

Then, without warning, I felt the presence of a second spirit. It was the crying woman, my grandmother Mary.

"Leave him alone, Will. This all belongs to him. It's time that he knows the truth."

"Silence, woman. Leave this place and never return!"

"How I wish I could. Perhaps someday."

In the blink of an eye, they were both gone. Holy shit, not one spirit, but two. It was now very obvious that I no longer needed a medium. I could see, hear, and communicate with spirits. This was not normal, was it? I just witnessed my dead grandparents arguing from beyond the grave. But why did Will want me to leave this place? I would have thought he'd be happy I had received The Thompson Family Farm. Maybe there's something here that he doesn't want me to know about? I don't know… it's all so confusing. Lisa, Kyle, Tina, Sue, the house, the spirits. Everything has been happening so quickly, I don't understand any of it. Maybe Grandpa Will is right. Maybe I should run away and never look back. I can't do that, though. I'm broke and my car won't start. It looks like I'm stuck here for a while.

Before returning to the house, I paused and looked around at the clearing. Even with so much shit going on in my life, it was exciting to know that this land belonged to me. After all these years, it is still part of the Thompson family. I knelt in the loose dirt and dug my hands under the surface. Making my hands the shape of shovels, I scooped up some of the soil and lifted it up to my face. The texture and the aroma were intoxicating. This was the foundation of life itself, for nothing edible would grow without this one crucial ingredient. I lowered my hands and released the soil I had been holding when something shiny caught my eye. What the hell was that? Try as I might, I couldn't find it. It was too tiny to find in all this dirt. Oh well, it couldn't have been that important.

I stood and brushed the soil from my hands and clothes. As I turned to head back home, the sound of a car horn was coming from the direction of my house. Maybe it was Sue? I ran back so she wouldn't think something bad had happened to me. But it already had.

Chapter 45

"**M**iss, you can't go in there! Miss!" James Bowen's new secretary tried to stop Lisa from entering his office.

"It's ok, he's expecting me." Lisa hurried past her and burst into her father's office.

"Sir, I tried to stop her, but she wouldn't listen to me."

"It's ok Jean, I'll take care of this."

Lisa slammed his office door shut and braced herself for another tongue lashing from James.

Massaging his temples, James had run out of patience with his daughter.

"Lisa, I thought you were leaving town. Why are you still here?"

Lisa knew that this may be the last time she would ever speak with her father, so this had to be good. Pausing much longer than she needed to, Lisa attempted to get her thoughts straight before speaking.

Finally, she said, "Daddy, we need to make things right with Jason."

With an amazed look on his face, James replied, "Make things right with Jason? Is that what you just said? Are you stupid, or what? What do you want to do, tell Jason the truth and then say '*Sorry, do you forgive us?*' It doesn't work that way. If we tell him the truth, we lose everything!"

"But *he's* already lost everything!"

"Lisa, get in your car and drive away. Go to Chicago, start your new life, and forget everything about your old one. Do it now, before you get hurt."

"Not until I tell Jason the truth first!"

James stood and grabbed Lisa by the shirt collar. "You're not going to tell him anything, do you understand?"

"Ouch, let go of me, you bastard!" Lisa tried to back away, but he wouldn't release his grip.

"I'm not going to jail because of you. Now get the hell out of Ventura and never come back!"

"Only after Jason knows the truth. We owe him that."

This was the last straw for James. He knew that this was cause for drastic measures. Wrapping his hands around the delicate neck of his daughter, he squeezed. This wasn't the first time he had tried to choke her, but this time was different. Unable to breathe, Lisa squirmed, which made things worse. The more she squirmed, the tighter his grip became. Coughing and gagging, but unable to get any words out, she tried to pry his hands from her neck, but his grip was too strong and would not release. Knowing that she was about to lose consciousness, she summoned all her remaining strength and reached her right hand into her purse.

"Daddy," she whispered. Pulling the handgun out of her purse and pushing the muzzle against his abdomen, she squeezed the trigger. As the bullet entered his midsection, he immediately released his grip and sank to his office floor.

"You bitch! You shot me. You really shot me!" His hands covered the wound as he tried to slow the bleeding.

He looked up at Lisa and was astonished to see her smiling down at him.

"Goodbye, Daddy," she said, as she fired another bullet into his forehead.

Feeling completely satisfied, she stepped into the bathroom to wash the splattered blood from her face. A quick brush of her hair and a touch-up of her makeup was all she needed. She reloaded her handgun, stepped over her father's body, and walked triumphantly out of Village Hall.

Now she had one more stop to make, and her mission would be complete.

Chapter 46

I ran back to the house, hoping to see Sue. I really wanted to sit down with her and share all the spiritual encounters I'd been having. She might not understand, and maybe she wouldn't believe me, but at least I would have someone to talk with. As I got close to the house, I could see that it wasn't Sue at all. It was Tina! What the hell did she want? I hadn't seen or heard from her since our ill-fated tryst. It was still mind blowing that a married woman would lie and cheat, and then just leave with no explanation.

Upon reaching her car, Tina stepped out and gave me a very cold stare. Her appearance had changed. She no longer looked like the beautiful girl next door. Now, she had the looks of the beautiful girl next door's ugly step-mother, complete with wrinkles on her face and bags under her eyes.

I smiled and said hello. She didn't respond.

"Would you like to come inside? I could make some coffee."

"Sure, why not?" Tina replied as she followed me inside.

I pulled out two k-cups and made the coffee while Tina sat at the kitchen table.

"How have you been?" I asked.

"Not good. I've been sick."

"Oh, I'm sorry to hear that. Did you have a cold?"

"No. It's called morning sickness."

My heart sank to the pit of my stomach when she said those words.

"Tina, why didn't you tell me you're married?"

"You never asked," was her reply.

"And why did Ken refer me to you, and not mention you're his wife?"

"No idea."

Her answers were brief and smug. I had a hard time believing anything she said.

"So, you're not sure who the father is yet, right?"

"Oh, it's definitely you. Ken is infertile. He can't father any children."

My anxiety kicked in and the thoughts in my mind were going a hundred miles per hour. How could I be so stupid? What now? Was I prepared to be a father? I couldn't even take care of myself. How was I supposed to support a child?

"Does he know you're pregnant?" I asked.

"Yes, he does. And he's not happy about it."

"So, what are you going to do with the baby?"

"That's a stupid question. What am I supposed to do with a baby? I'm going to have it, of course. Ken and I are going to raise it, and you are going to support it."

She had obviously thought this through.

"Tina, I'll do what I can, but you have to understand that I'm broke. I don't have a job, my savings are wiped, and my credit cards are maxed out."

Tina began strolling through the kitchen and dining room, examining every nook and cranny.

"I don't know, Jay. It looks like you're doing pretty darn good."

"What are you saying? You want me to sell my house? I just moved in here, and haven't finished unpacking yet."

"No, you can keep your damned house. I just want some land. Say, maybe 30 acres or so?"

Why did everyone want some of my land? What makes my land so valuable? I didn't want to be giving away any of my land, but on the other hand, if that's all I needed to do to support my child, it might be worth it.

"I'll have to think about it. Let's wait until the baby is born, and we can run a paternity test. If the baby is mine, we'll figure out how I can support it."

Tina's eyes turned red, and anger filled her facial features.

"This needs to be done now, for the longer we wait, the more you're going to owe me."

It was unbelievable. She was trying to use a fetus as a bargaining chip.

"Nope. We're not sure I'm the father, and honestly, I don't even know if I can believe that you're actually pregnant."

Reaching into her handbag, Tina pulled out some papers that appeared to be legal documents drawn up by an attorney. She laid the papers on the kitchen table and handed me a ballpoint pen.

"I already told you that you're the only guy I've been with, other than Ken. If you know what's good for you, you'll sign these papers. It's only thirty acres. You already have more land than you know what to do with."

If I know what's good for me? What the hell was that supposed to mean? Damn it, I was so tired of being treated this way. I'd had enough and couldn't take any more crap. I grabbed the papers from the table and tore them into small pieces.

"Get out! Get the hell out of my house and stay out! What is wrong with you? You and your husband are sick people, and I will not play your sick games!"

I expected Tina to run for the door, but she remained calm. Reaching into her bag, she pulled out a second set of papers, identical to the first set.

"I thought you might react in that manner. That's why I brought along a second set of documents. I also brought something else to help with your decision." Tina reached into her bag a third time and pulled out a Ruger .22 caliber handgun. She aimed it at my face and said, "You will sign these papers today, one way or another."

At that moment, I knew fear...actual fear. I knew what it meant to see my life flash before my eyes. So much for being tough and standing my ground. I was going to sign the damn papers, anyway.

"Okay, Tina. Calm down, I'll sign. Give me a pen and I'll sign."

Tina had a victorious sneer on her face. She had accomplished her objectives. Now Tina, Ken, and the baby could use my land however they wished. I still couldn't understand what they were going to do with thirty acres of rough, rocky land.

I read the fine print, signed by the X, and handed the papers back to Tina. Casually glancing over her left shoulder, I had a clear view of the back porch. And who was standing there with gun in hand? It was Lisa. The back door swung open, as Lisa stepped forward and yelled out, "Drop It!"

I closed my eyes and fell to the floor. Although Lisa had lied and hurt me in the past, I truly believe she had changed her ways and was seeking some type of redemption. The sound of gunfire and a loud, blood-curdling scream filled the air, along with the bitter odor of gunpowder.

"Jay, grab her gun!" yelled Lisa.

I opened my eyes to see a handgun lying on the floor, and Tina applying pressure to her right forearm, trying to slow the bleeding.

"Throw it in the sink, Jay."

I did as Lisa told me to do.

"Have a seat, bitch!" Lisa said slyly.

Tina was a mess. Wiping her tears with blood-soaked hands was only spreading the redness all over her face.

"Go to hell, Lisa."

"After you," was Lisa's reply.

"Oh my God," I yelled. "I can't believe you shot her!"

"Why not? She would have shot you."

I hadn't thought of it that way. Still, I couldn't just let her suffer. I handed Tina a towel and used a wet washcloth to wipe the blood from her face.

"Maybe we should call 9-1-1. She said she's pregnant, and she is bleeding pretty badly."

"She'll be okay, and I can guarantee you she isn't pregnant. Isn't that right, Tina?"

Tina glared at Lisa, with defeat written all over her face.

I asked Lisa how she could be so sure of Tina's lie.

"Easy. If she really was pregnant, she would have waited until the baby was born, had a paternity test done, and let a judge decide the amount of support. Instead, she threatened you at gunpoint."

"I'm sorry, Jay." Tina began. "It was all Ken's idea. I never should have listened to him."

With a huge grin on her face, Lisa proudly proclaimed, "At least you'll never have to listen to another one of his crazy ideas."

Tina looked confused. "No? Why do you say that?"

Lisa paused, enjoying every second of anticipation filling the room. "Because he's lying on his office floor, in a pool of blood, with two bullets in his chest."

Sadness filled the face of Tina, as she struggled to get the words out. "You killed my husband? Why? Why would you do that?"

"Sorry, sweetie, but he had it coming. Today is Jay's retribution day, and I'm just helping the process."

Suddenly, Tina jumped up from her seat and pushed me out of the way. As she screamed the word, "Nooo!!!" she ran for the sink. Lisa was way ahead of her, though. It was as if she was expecting it, almost daring Tina to go for it. Although she made it to the kitchen sink, Tina didn't have a chance to turn and exact revenge. Lisa calmly squeezed off two rounds into the back of Tina's skull. Death was instantaneous, as Tina fell to the ground.

"Lisa, stop it! Why are you doing this?" It was obvious that Lisa had gone insane. There was no other way to explain what was happening. Now, I wondered if she was done, or was she going to continue killing? Maybe I was going to be next? If so, it would finally be the end of the Thompson family in Ventura.

"I'm doing this for you, Jay. I know this must be extremely hard to understand, but I can explain. Let's go in the other room, away from all this blood, and I'll tell you everything."

I followed her into the living room and prayed that Lisa would find it in her heart to let me live.

Chapter 47

I took a seat on the couch, positioned directly across from Lisa, who was comfortably seated in a plush recliner. This was the first time I sat in the living room of my new home. Watching Lisa grip the pistol in her hands made me wonder if it would be the last. I still wasn't sure what had happened to Lisa, but she was definitely off her rocker. Did she really want to make amends with me, or was I going to be her next victim? I played it cool and listened to what she had to say.

"Your house is beautiful, Jay! I absolutely love it!"

"Thanks Lisa, I appreciate that."

We sat there for several minutes, watching each other and smiling. It was an understatement to say that it was awkward.

"So, you're probably wondering what's going on here, eh?"

"Well, yeah, the thought did cross my mind." With a dead body in my kitchen, and my ex-fiance pointing a gun at me, this was definitely not an average day in my life.

"I'm sorry. I didn't mean to scare you. Jay, me and several other people have lied you to for a long time. Most of your suspicions and intuitions have been correct, but you don't know the half of it. I want to go away and start a new life, but I know I could never be happy until I correct the mistakes I made in the past. So, that's what I'm doing today."

"Lisa, just because certain people have lied to me in the past, it doesn't make it okay to kill them. I don't want that kind of guilt on my shoulders."

Lisa placed her gun on the arm of the recliner, but it was still pointed at me, which made things very tense. "I'm not trying to make you feel any kind of guilt. That's the last thing I would want."

"Okay, so what *do* you want?"

"I have so much to tell you, but not a lot of time. Just know that everything I'm about to tell you is the absolute truth. It's all information that I have witnessed to be true, or have been told by reputable sources. You won't get any more lies from me."

"Lisa, really, you don't need to tell me anything." I just wanted her, and that gun, far away from me.

"Believe me, you'll thank me once you know the truth. So, let's get started, shall we?"

I felt like I was back in high school, about to sit through an hour long biology lecture.

"Everyone in town loved and respected your great-grandparents, Caleb and Flora. They were the type of people who were always willing to help their neighbors. Flora was an excellent teacher, Caleb was involved in local politics, and they were both very active in their church. The one thing they struggled with, though, was their ability to be good parents. Will was their only child, and they spoiled him rotten. Many old-timers I spoke with remembered him as selfish and rude."

"Okay, I know little about Grandpa Will, but the stories told about him haven't been good."

Lisa checked the time and kept a close watch out the front door. It was almost as if she was waiting for a train.

"Will Thompson was Ventura's All-American boy. He had dreams of being a professional baseball player with a squeaky clean persona. That should guarantee him he would never have to work another day in his life. Will absolutely hated farming and resented having to help his father work in the fields. With a full scholarship to the University of Illinois, Will could concentrate on baseball without having to worry about farming. Unfortunately, he was drafted into the army immediately after graduating from high school. He told friends and family that he enlisted, though. That way, he made himself appear to be an honorable and patriotic young man."

"Lisa, is there something in the front yard you're looking for?" I asked.

Lisa stood and began pacing back and forth in the living room.

"Nope. So anyway, Will was injured fighting in World War 2, and that was the end of his baseball career. After the war ended, he reluctantly returned home to work on the farm, and wound up marrying his high school sweetheart, Mary Kallas."

"You probably think I'm crazy, but the spirit of Mary was there the day we went to the Ventura Diner. Do you remember that day?"

"Yeah, how could I forget? I'm sorry Jay. I was a total jerk to you that day."

Lisa's hands began to tremble.

"Anyway, the downfall of your family began when Caleb purchased some additional land, down in back of his existing fields. Business had been good, and with Will back home to help him, Caleb looked to increase profits. I'm not sure what he planted in those fields, but I know that my great grandfather, Thomas Bowen, was very nosy and began sneaking around Caleb's property to see what had been planted there."

I could remember my dad telling me stories about Thomas and TJ, two of the nastiest men to ever live in Ventura. Lisa's father, James, was cut from the same mold as his ancestors. Thank God I didn't marry Lisa. What a screwed up family I'd have to deal with.

Lisa continued, "So, Thomas found what he was looking for, as did your Grandpa Will. It turned man against man, neighbor against neighbor, and father against son. Thomas practically begged Caleb and Flora to sell him those fields. Will tried to convince Caleb to quit farming and use the land for other purposes. However, Caleb refused both men because he loved farming. That's all he ever wanted to do, and unfortunately, it was the very thing that ended his life."

"Lisa, I don't get it. What was so important that it created all of this conflict?"

Lisa looked like she was ready to cry. She knelt down beside me and wrapped her arms around me. "I'm so sorry, Jay. I didn't want to be the one to tell you this, but no one else had the balls to do it. So, if you're ready, hold on to your hat, because I'm about to tell you the craziest part of this story!"

Chapter 48

"**O**kay, Lisa, I'm ready. Tell me the craziest part of this story."

"It's gold, Jay! Gold!"

"What's gold?"

"Your land! It's a gold mine!"

I didn't know what to say. This woman had clearly lost her mind. All I could do was look at her with pity in my heart. If I could only get that gun away from her, I'd call 9-1-1 and request an ambulance take her to Crandall County Psychiatric Hospital.

Lisa had a puzzled look on her face. "You don't believe me, do you?"

"Lisa, there are no gold mines in Illinois. Why don't you hand me your pistol, and I'll call some people who can help you."

Lisa took a step back and aimed the gun at my face. "Don't move, Jay. I know it sounds crazy, but didn't I say that I would tell you the truth? Well, that's exactly what I'm doing. So, sit there, shut up and allow me to tell you the rest of the story, okay? After this is over, talk to Sheriff Booker. He'll confirm everything I'm telling you."

I really didn't have a choice, so I shut my mouth and let Lisa continue to speak. Maybe she wasn't as crazy as I thought. Couldn't hurt to listen, right?

"So, I don't blame you for being skeptical...I would be, too. There is a small section of land located right in the center of the thirty acres that Caleb purchased in 1950 that contains a very dense vein of gold, which comes right to the surface. It is unlike anything you've ever seen. Old-timers used to swear those fields would sparkle when the sun rose in the morning. My father just recently pulled his equipment out and filled in the mine. If you see an area of loose soil with no vegetation, that's where the gold is."

Holy shit, maybe this isn't as crazy as it sounds.

"This is why the Bowen family and your Grandpa Will wanted this land so badly. They knew it would make them rich."

"Lisa, you said that farming ended Caleb's life? I don't get it. What did you mean by that?"

"Once again, Jay, I didn't want to be the one to tell you this, but you need to know the truth. Will desperately wanted Caleb to quit farming and begin mining. It would have meant no more backbreaking work, no more struggles paying bills, and the whole family would be rich. Caleb wouldn't hear of it, though. Farming is all he knew, farming is what he loved. Well, one day in the summer of 1953, Will gave Caleb an ultimatum. Stop farming and start mining, or Will was going to leave. Caleb basically told Will to do what he felt was right, so Will picked up a shovel and beat Caleb in the head with it, killing him instantly. He disposed of the body in Lake Menderville, making it look like an accident."

"Holy shit Lisa, I saw this happen in a vision, but I assumed that Thomas Bowen was the murderer. Who'd have thought that my grandfather would have killed his own father?"

Lisa replied, "My great-grandfather, Thomas, was a lot of things, but he wasn't a murderer."

Lisa lowered her gun, knowing that she now had my undivided attention.

"Unfortunately, it didn't stop there. The following spring, Will tried to convince Flora to quit farming, but she wouldn't hear of it. She knew Caleb's wishes and would do everything in her power to carry them out. Will finally ran out of patience in May 1954, when he smashed his mother's skull on a large rock in her garden. Will threw a rake on the ground next to the body to make it look like an accident."

What kind of sick, demented person would kill his own

parents for money? This makes no sense to me. Was my entire life a lie? Were all of my beliefs, all my memories just made up?

"Tell me more, Lisa. You've gone this far. Might as well tell me everything. What other lies were told? Who else was murdered?"

"Okay, when Will killed Flora, he thought there were no witnesses. Little did he know that his wife, Mary, was in the barn next to Flora's garden. Imagine what she felt when she witnessed her husband kill his own mother? To top it off, Mary was pregnant with your father at the time. Fear gripped Will when he found out his wife had witnessed his latest slaying. So, shortly after your dad was born, Mary went missing. No one ever found out where she went, but you get the picture."

It was sad, but I got the picture, and it was clear. My grandfather was a serial killer who had an obsession with money.

Lisa continued, "That's when Will quit farming and built the fence around the farm. I guess it was a combination of hiding the gold and anything else that might be buried here. So anyway, Will had an affair with my Great Aunt Hazel, and they had a child, David, who was Tina's father. After Will passed away, my grandfather, TJ Bowen, found a way to steal your father's identity. By paying off certain local politicians, he took control of the land, mined the gold, and paid the taxes. They told your father that they seized the farm for back taxes, even though he was still the legal owner."

"So, your family did a real good job of stealing from my father. And from me, for that matter. How could you allow this to happen, Lisa? Didn't you love me?"

Lisa bowed her head in shame. "I wanted to tell you, Jay, but if I had, my life would have been in jeopardy. I still love you...just wish things could have been different."

I took a moment to think of any other unanswered questions I had. Only two popped into my head. "Who set the fire that killed my family?"

Lisa couldn't look me in the eye. "I don't know. Probably some ex-con my father hired. He wouldn't tell me. Your dad had been asking a lot of questions about the farm. My father felt he needed to be eliminated."

My hatred for the Bowen family grew more intense with each word we spoke, but I needed an answer to one more question. "So, why did both you and Tina want to have my children?"

"Caleb had a clause added to his will that stated the farm must remain in the family forever. If there are no descendents left in the family line, the property ownership goes to the State of Illinois. That would have meant losing the gold mine. My father could hide things from you, but he couldn't hide legal matters from the State. Since you were the last of the Thompsons, we needed to create an heir so we wouldn't lose everything. Unfortunately, Tina and Ken had the same plan that my father had."

"Nice plan. Sleep with me to create an heir, and then do away with me. I guess my role would be as a sperm donor. God, now I know what a praying mantis feels like."

"I'm sorry, Jay. I know how hard this must be for you. The truth had to be told, though. Now, we can both have a fresh start and get on with our lives. I've emailed all the tax records, receipts, and photos that you'll need to sue my family. They stole millions of dollars of gold from you. Get yourself a good lawyer, and you'll be rich."

Gun or no gun, I approached Lisa, wound up and slapped her face as hard as I could. She cried out in pain, but I couldn't hold it in any longer. "You think it's as easy as that?" I screamed. "No house, no gold mine, and no amount of money will ever bring my family back! I've literally lost everything. All I've ever wanted was to have a family, and to be loved. Is that too much to ask for, Lisa? Is it?! Instead, I wind up with not one, but two women who only wanted me for my sperm. Now one is dead, and the other is fucking crazy! I'd really like to get some revenge on your father, though. He's the most to blame here."

Lisa wiped the tears from her eyes. "I already took care of him."

"You mean you...?"

Lisa nodded and whispered, "Yep. Two bullets. One in the gut and the other in the head."

"Holy shit!"

I sat on the couch and covered my face with my hands, not wanting to see anything or anyone. I just wanted to leave Crandall County and never look back. Insanity was running rampant here, and I wanted nothing more to do with it.

Just then, the back door opened. Lisa spun around and checked to make sure her gun had ammo left in it. Looking toward the kitchen, she yelled, "Who's out there?"

"Lisa, it's only me, Sheriff Booker. I'm coming in...don't shoot me!"

Booker gingerly stepped around the corner into the living room. He had his pistol drawn and aimed at Lisa. She, in turn, had hers fixed on the Sheriff.

"Put the gun down, Lisa. Let's sit down and talk."

"You're too late, Sheriff. I've finished talking. Jay knows all about the lies, the murders, and the gold. I told him everything."

"That's good. He needed to know all about it. Now, please put the gun down."

Lisa glanced at me momentarily, then returned her eyes to Sheriff Booker. In an odd way, I felt sorry for her. Here was a beautiful, intelligent woman who could have the world at her feet. Instead, her father drove her to insanity. She had less to live for than I did. The moment that thought went through my mind, Lisa whispered to me, "Goodbye, Jay."

As she raised the gun to her temple, I shouted, "No, Lisa!" but to no avail. She squeezed the trigger, and blood splattered as she fell to the floor.

Chapter 49

"Hey."

"Oh, hey Sue. How are ya?"

Sue let herself in my front door and quickly noticed the bed sheets covering my living room furniture. The blood stains would have to be sanded out of the hardwood floor.

"I'm okay. What's up? How come you haven't returned my phone calls?"

It had been three months since the killings occurred, but I was still having major issues with anxiety and depression. A new therapist in town had prescribed several medications, but they had helped little.

"It has nothing to do with you, Sue. I just haven't felt like talking with anyone."

"Okay. Do you want me to leave?"

"No. It's good that you're here. I wanted to tell you I'm going away for a while."

What the hell is wrong with me? Standing before me was a good woman whom I've known for many years, and I trust completely. Yet, all I want to do is run away.

"Going away? Where are you going?"

"Seattle. There's a psychic school there that I've enrolled in. I used to think that mediums were full of shit, but lately I've realized that it's the only thing that I'm any good at. I'd like to pursue it as a career, and try to improve my mediumship abilities."

"I see. So, how long will you be gone?"

This was the hard part. I didn't want to throw away any

chance at finding happiness with Sue, but I needed to get away. Far away. Everywhere I looked, I saw death. Violent murders are common on tv, but to actually witness not one, but two in one day has burned it into my mind. Will these visions ever go away? God, I hope so. Besides the murders that I witnessed, I was still dealing with the killings of my grandfather and the bloodshed that Lisa had caused before she came to visit me on her fateful day.

"The school lasts for six months. After that, I'm not sure."

Sue strolled slowly through the living and dining rooms of my house, pausing every two or three steps, trying to force some words out of her mouth. It was the first time I can remember that Sue was speechless.

Finally, I changed the subject. "Did you see my new car in the driveway? It's just like yours, only I went for a white one."

Sue tried to act interested. "Yeah, it's nice. Very sharp looking. So, I take it you're okay with money?"

"Yep. I handed off all the paperwork from Lisa to my lawyer. The Bowen family knew they were guilty, so they didn't fight it. I agreed to not press criminal charges and two weeks later, I had a check for eight million dollars."

"Oh my God! How does it feel to be a millionaire?"

"It's nice not having to worry about money, but I'd much rather have my family back. By the way, how much money do I owe you?"

Sue couldn't hold it in any longer. Grabbing me by the shirt collar, she began shouting, "I don't want your damn money! I just want you! Can't you see that?"

I didn't realize her feelings were so intense.

"Go to your school, Jay. Take as much time as you need, but please come back to me. We lost each other once. Let's not do it again!"

I held her in my arms for what seemed like an hour while she sobbed uncontrollably. Finally, we kissed and said our goodbyes. I wasn't sure if I would return, but I promised Sue that I would try to forget the past, so we could have a future.

* * *

The lengthy driveway of the Ventura Cemetery seemed almost welcoming to me. This is where I could go for my family 'reunions', although I was confident my family didn't live here. I knew they were alive and thriving in a special corner of heaven.

Roughly a dozen mourners had gathered around the graves of Caleb and Flora, forming a tight circle while holding hands, creating a bustling atmosphere. As I moved closer, the mourners were not what they appeared to be. This was my family. The spirits of my family, and they were all smiling. Even Grandma Mary had stopped crying. There was no more sadness, no more pain. The truth had finally been told, and the farm was back in the hands of the Thompson family. Now, I just needed to get my act together and rebuild the farm for future generations.

I was about to leave when a new spirit emerged from the center of their circle. It was Lisa! She, too, was smiling. The energy I was receiving assured me they had accepted and welcomed her into the family. She was one of us now.

Returning to my car, I said farewell to my family and to Ventura. The long drive to Seattle, and the hopes of growing closer to the spirit world, were exciting. Maybe I could put the past behind me and clear my mind. The future was finally looking brighter.

Made in the USA
Monee, IL
14 January 2025

76716381R00104